## John Creasey – M

Born in Surrey, England in 1908 i
were nine children, John Creasey &
teller and international sensation. His more than 600 crime, mystery and thriller titles have now sold 80 million copies in 25 languages. These include many popular series such as *Gideon of Scotland Yard*, *The Toff*, *Dr Palfrey* and *The Baron*.

Creasy wrote under many pseudonyms, explaining that booksellers had complained he totally dominated the 'C' section in stores. They included:

*Gordon Ashe, M E Cooke, Norman Deane, Robert Caine Frazer, Patrick Gill, Michael Halliday, Charles Hogarth, Brian Hope, Colin Hughes, Kyle Hunt, Abel Mann, Peter Manton, J J Marric, Richard Martin, Rodney Mattheson, Anthony Morton* and *Jeremy York*.

Never one to sit still, Creasey had a strong social conscience, and stood for Parliament several times, along with founding the One Party Alliance which promoted the idea of government by a coalition of the best minds from across the political spectrum.

He also founded the British Crime Writers' Association, which to this day celebrates outstanding crime writing. The Mystery Writers of America bestowed upon him the Edgar Award for best novel and then in 1969 the ultimate Grand Master Award. John Creasey's stories are as compelling today as ever.

## INPECTOR WEST SERIES

Inspector West Takes Charge
Inspector West Leaves Town (Also published as: Go Away to Murder)
Inspector West at Home (Also published as: An Apostle of Gloom)
Inspector West Regrets
Holiday for Inspector West
Battle for Inspector West
Triumph for Inspector West (Also published as: The Case Against Paul Raeburn)
Inspector West Kicks Off (Also published as: Sport for Inspector West)
Inspector West Alone
Inspector West Cries Wolf (Also published as: The Creepers)
A Case for Inspector West (Also published as: The Figure in the Dusk)
Puzzle for Inspector West (Also published as: The Dissemblers)
Inspector West at Bay (Also published as: The Case of the Acid Throwers)
A Gun for Inspector West (Also published as: Give a Man a Gun)
Send Inspector West (Also published as: Send Superintendent West)
A Beauty for Inspector West (Also published as: The Beauty Queen Killer)
Inspector West Makes Haste (Also published as: Murder Makes Haste)
Two for Inspector West (Also published as: Murder: One, Two, Three)
Parcels for Inspector West (Also published as: Death of a Postman)
A Prince for Inspector West (Also published as: Death of a Assassin)
Accident for Inspector West (Also published as: Hit and Run)
Find Inspector West (Also published as: Doorway to Death)
Murder, London - New York
Strike for Death (Also published as: The Killing Strike)
Death of a Racehorse
The Case of the Innocent Victims
Murder on the Line
Death in Cold Print
The Scene of the Crime
Policeman's Dread
Hang the Little Man
Look Three Ways at Murder
Murder, London - Australia
Murder, London - South Africa
The Executioners
So Young to Burn
Murder, London - Miami
A Part for a Policeman
Alibi (Also published as: Alibi for Inspector West)
A Splinter of Glass
The Theft of Magna Carta
The Extortioners
A Sharp Rise in Crime

# Hit And Run

## (Accident for Inspector West)

## John Creasey

Copyright © 1957 John Creasey Literary Management Ltd.
© 2014 House of Stratus

All rights reserved. No part of this publication may be reproduced, stored in a retrieval system, or transmitted, in any form, or by any means (electronic, mechanical, photocopying, recording, or otherwise), without the prior permission of the publisher. Any person who does any unauthorised act in relation to this publication may be liable to criminal prosecution and civil claims for damages.

The right of John Creasey to be identified as the author of this work has been asserted.

This edition published in 2014 by House of Stratus, an imprint of Stratus Books Ltd., Lisandra House, Fore Street, Looe, Cornwall, PL13 1AD, U.K.
www.houseofstratus.com

Typeset by House of Stratus.

A catalogue record for this book is available from the British Library and the Library of Congress.

ISBN 07551-3575-X
EAN 978-07551-3575-2

This book is sold subject to the condition that it shall not be lent, resold, hired out, or otherwise circulated without the publisher's express prior consent in any form of binding, or cover, other than the original as herein published and without a similar condition being imposed on any subsequent purchaser, or bona fide possessor.

This is a fictional work and all characters are drawn from the author's imagination. Any resemblance or similarities to persons either living or dead are entirely coincidental.

## Chapter One

## The First Crime

The first crime was committed four years and the second six months before anyone began to suspect any crime at all – except in the most general sense of the word. True, it was actually used several times, both when the body was discovered and at the inquest, but that was in the sense which few took really seriously. Most meant "crime" in the sense that they would mean "it's a crying shame".

Chief Inspector West of the Yard, who was later to investigate the whole series, read about the second crime in the *Evening Globe*, the only paper of any size which reported it in any detail. He read about it casually as of any hit-and-run accident, and when his wife said, "Oh, do put that paper down and get on with your dinner," he obeyed, and did not give the affair another serious thought.

At least, not then.

The second crime had been committed that very morning. Like this:

Eunice Marsden was torn between the desire to catch the earliest bus possible and reach Oxford Street in time for the New Year's sales, and taking Meg to school, which was on the way, before going to the West End. The best of the buys would be gone by then, but so would the worst of the fray. She was leaning towards the second, weaker course, when Mrs. Bray arrived early.

Mrs. Bray was comparatively new to the Marsden household, and Eunice was dangerously near the stage of persuading herself that at last she had a "treasure". Her experience with dailies had convinced her that most of them chattered only to deceive, and she was reluctant even to admit the possibility of a find to her husband. Mrs. Bray's arrival at half-past eight, although she was not due until nine o'clock, seemed to put the seal on her sterling worth, and it made up Eunice Marsden's mind.

The daily woman turned into the gate of the small, detached house near Kingston-on-Thames, small and rather plump, fifty or so, wearing a grey coat, a grey felt hat and a woollen muffler tight about her neck, to keep out the piercing cold. Her eyes were watering in the wind as she walked briskly along the crazy-paving path towards the front door, and Meg, who was a kind of human radar, came tearing down the stairs from her room.

"M's Bay," she said, "here's M's Bay."

Eunice hesitated between two corrections, and chose the simpler.

"Bray," she said, "there's an 'r'. Bray."

"She's here," declared Meg, eagerly, "may I open the door, Mummy?"

She could just reach. She had long, dark, wavy hair which soon became a mess, pale, skinny arms and pale, skinny legs – and a measure of training which was likely to stand her in good stead later; for she waited for permission before trying to open the door.

Mrs. Bray's footsteps sounded briskly in the porch.

"Yes, go on," said Eunice.

Meg stretched up and tightened her lips and pushed with a rigid forefinger. The bell rang. Meg grunted with the effort, but her mother didn't go to her aid. The bell rang again, just as the catch slid back and the door sagged open.

"Don't push, Mrs. Bray," Eunice called out.

"Oh, it's Meg," said Mrs. Bray, as the door opened wider. She smiled down at the child, cheerfully. She never fussed her or seemed likely to spoil her. "Thank you, Meg, and how are you this morning?"

Meg chattered.

"Bless you for being early," Eunice said. "I think I'll just put on a hat and coat and catch the first bus I can for the West End sales, if you'll take Meg along to school."

"Yes, of course I will," said Mrs. Bray, "that's why I'm early. You said yesterday you were in half a mind to see if you could get a new coat and an outfit for Meg."

That hadn't been meant as a hint, and in any case, it didn't matter now. Mrs. Bray gave her subdued, almost tight-lipped little smile and went through to the kitchen, Meg following, and Eunice went upstairs, long legs taking them two at a time, her mind already on what clothes she was going to look for. She was downstairs again in less than ten minutes, as smart as three-year-old tweed suit and a small black hat would allow.

"Good-bye, Meg!"

"'Bye, Mummy." Meg, who never seemed to stop hurrying, came running. They kissed.

"Be good, now."

"Ess."

"Good-bye, Mrs. Bray, and thank—"

"Expect you when I see you," said Mrs. Bray, "and I'll be at the school for Meg at a quarter-past twelve, so don't break your neck to hurry back."

"I won't." Eunice smiled, and her smile could be radiant. Mrs. Bray's was still a little set, almost reluctant, as if she was not used to smiling.

Eunice hurried along the street towards the main road and the bus stop, thinking more about the daily woman than about Meg. It was easy to imagine that Mrs. Bray had known plenty of trouble, as easy to believe that her life had been hard, but she had said very little about herself, except that the old lady for whom she had worked for years had died, leaving her a thousand pounds – and freedom.

"But I couldn't bear doing nothing for long," she told Eunice, "I've always liked being busy, Mrs. Marsden."

"And children don't worry you?"

"It'll be a pleasant change," Mrs. Bray had said. "It doesn't do to spend too much time with the very old, that's what I've come to believe."

That was easy to say.

There was Meg much of the time, and the two boys, aged eleven and fourteen, home at week-ends; they were weekly boarders at as good a school as the Marsdens could manage. Three week-ends had passed, and neither the boys nor Mrs. Bray had shown much outward enthusiasm for each other, but they seemed to get along.

The daily work of the house was often finished earlier than usual, Eunice had time for an afternoon nap, and was bright and fresh in the evenings. If things went on like this, then "treasure" would be the only word.

Eunice found herself still thinking of the daily woman, and when she was near Oxford Street, in a bus jammed full with hopeful bargain-hunters, she realised that she hadn't felt a moment's anxiety about leaving Meg. Usually she would be worried in case the child slipped away from her companion and ran into the road; at five and a bit there was very little road sense. She would not slip away from Mrs. Bray, Eunice thought; it just wouldn't happen.

The doors of Harridges were open, but the long queue of shoppers hadn't all gone in. It was going to be a lusty scramble, but if she could pick up one or two real bargains it would be worth it.

She was nearly pushed off the bus.

"Elbows out and head down," she said to herself, and smiled, and was soon hustled along.

It was then twenty minutes past nine – when Meg and Mrs. Bray should be leaving the house for the school, which was only ten minutes' walk away.

"I don't want to have my hair tied at the back," said Meg, flatly, "I want it tied at the front."

"So you do?"

"Yes," said Meg, and then seeing a glint in Mrs. Bray's grey eyes, added hastily: "Please, M's Bay."

"Well, you've too much hair to have it tied at the front," said Mrs. Bray, practically. "I'll bet your mother's told you that plenty of times. We'll try it at the side, and see how it does." She tied the bow of pink ribbon neatly and briskly, wasted no time patting it, and went to get her coat. Soon they were in the street, hand in hand, the wind behind them and not very noticeable or worrying. Meg skipped every few paces, to keep up with Mrs. Bray. As they drew near the main road, a white cat slunk across their path, and into the road.

"Oo—" Meg tried to free herself.

"If he's there when we're coming home you can see if he'll let you stroke him," promised Mrs. Bray. "Just now we're in a hurry."

Meg glanced up at her, owlishly, and then submitted. The cat vanished behind a hedge. Two buses and a tradesman's van went by, just as Mrs. Bray and Meg passed a car which was parked at the side of the road, with a man at the wheel. It was a black car of a popular make and size, with nothing at all remarkable about it. The man at the wheel was dressed in charcoal grey, with a muffler and a trilby hat; he appeared to be reading a newspaper.

Two hundred yards farther along was a zebra crossing, where the couple would cross; the school was in a side street only a few minutes' walk from the opposite side. Two mothers went over with their children, but no pedestrians were in sight when Mrs. Bray and Meg neared it. The engine of the car started up, the self-starter squeaking in the morning's cold, but Mrs. Bray didn't give that a thought, and did not even glance round towards the car until she reached the kerb at the zebra.

Some way off, there was a cyclist.

Out of sight, there was a bus with a noisy engine.

Mrs. Bray held the child's hand tightly, and waited for the car – but for once a driver did not try to beat the pedestrian. He slowed down, and waved them on to the crossing with the nose of the car only a few yards away.

"Now hold my hand tight and hurry," Mrs. Bray said in that nearly severe tone, "and don't skip or jump." She glanced in the other direction to make sure that the road was clear, and stepped on to the zebra.

She heard the sudden roar of the car engine.

Startled, she turned her head.

The car was coming towards them; *hurtling,* with the engine rasping in low gear. She saw the eyes of the driver, glittering, saw that his mouth was wide open, and knew that he was here to kill her.

There was no time to save herself.

She snatched her hand from Meg's, and thrust it vigorously into the small of the child's back, pushing her forward with such strength that Meg was flung out of the path of the car.

Then, the car struck.

The child was on the ground, gathering her breath for a great scream of pain and shock. The cyclist, almost unsighted, saw only the child. The car engine roared again, and the car went on; then the cyclist saw Mrs. Bray, as she lay unmoving.

"Death must have been instantaneous," said the doctor who was there five minutes later. "The wheel crushed her skull. Yes, get her away. Now, what about that child?"

Eunice Marsden congratulated herself, for it had been a much better trip than she had hoped. She had a two-piece which was worth every penny of twenty guineas, but had cost her nine, and that alone would have justified the journey. Then there were Meg's clothes, perhaps rather more of them than she would have bought at ordinary prices, but—

She turned the corner of Sheldrake Street, and saw the headmistress's car outside the house, but did not see Meg. Quite suddenly, fear took hold of her. *Meg.* She forgot her tiredness and began to run. What was this about, where was Mrs. Bray, what could—"

Meg was getting out of the car; there was plaster on her chin and nose.

"Meg!" her mother called. "Meg, what is it?" Then she stopped calling, and also stopped running.

She would never forget the way Meg looked at her, or the tone of her daughter's voice as she told her the simple truth.

"M's Bay dead," she announced. "A man knocked her down in a car."

The headmistress came hurrying.

"It's a crime," she began. "He ought to hang, he—"

Later, the coroner solemnly agreed that it was a crime.

He adjourned the inquest to allow the police to make further efforts to trace the car and its driver, but without success.

The only witness was the cyclist, who had seen everything for the back, and could only say emphatically that the engine had suddenly made a lot of noise. He had not been able to see the registration number, because his eyes had been watering so much from the wind.

He was that kind of witness.

The police filed the case, for to the Criminal Investigation Department, hit and run was a crime of the worst kind. Yet this one did not appear to merit more than a few short paragraphs before it was forgotten by the newspapers. Mrs. Bray was too colourless to make news.

One of the odd things about the affair was that very little was discovered about Mrs. Bray, except that she had lived in one room in Putney, that she had looked after an elderly woman for twelve years, that she had inherited some money – it did not seem worth worrying to find out how much – and had left a total of nearly seven thousand pounds.

There was no will, and no one came forward to claim the estate.

Month after month this case came up for review at the Division – one on the perimeter of the Metropolitan Police area – and at Scotland Yard. Roger West himself studied all the reports, as a matter of routine. He could find nothing fresh about Mrs. Bray, nothing to indicate whether the driver had simply lost his head after striking her, or whether he had deliberately run her down. The second was so unlikely, in the Yard's experience, that it was not even suggested.

West did discover one thing, which he regarded wryly. The one brief moment of glory which had lighted up the drab if useful life of Mrs. Bray had possessed a bitter twist of irony. Four years before her own death, she had been a witness in an inquest on a younger woman who had been killed in a road accident. Simply because he placed thoroughness at the top of his list of "qualities required by a police officer" West asked the Superintendent of the Division in which that accident had occurred for details.

"Straightforward enough job," he was told, that same afternoon. "A young woman got off a bus and stepped round the back of it without looking where she was going. No one's fault but her own. Several witnesses available. This Mrs. Bray was just behind her, that's why she was so reliable. Worst thing was that the woman didn't die quickly, although she was badly injured – died over a year later. Death directly attributable to the accident, no argument about that."

It would be easy to ask for more details, the name of the driver and of other witnesses, but there seemed no point in doing so. At least Mrs. Bray had died instantaneously, the suffering was too often the worst part of accident tragedies.

"What kind of car was it?" Roger asked.

"A Jag. Only doing twenty-five or thirty, though, the driver couldn't be blamed in any way. Right opposite the place I'm speaking from, too."

Just an accident, mused Roger as he thanked the Superintendent, and rang off. They were part of the risks of life, like poliomyelitis, cancer and war.

The absurd idea that the same car might have been involved was stillborn, for the car which had killed Mrs. Bray had been of 10 or 12 horse-power, certainly no larger. The witness had put the crowning touch to his inept performance by saying only that it had been a "popular" make of car, certainly a small one; well, no larger than medium-sized. No one would confuse that with a Jaguar.

It was a poor show for Mrs. Bray, with her seven thousand pounds and her snug job with the Marsdens. Her earlier post must have been well paid, or else she had inherited a biggish sum – or even won a small fortune on the pools.

At that time her seven thousand pounds seemed to have no special significance.

The next crime was not even remotely concerned, as far as anyone could judge, with accidents of any kind.

## Chapter Two

## The Second Crime

Rosemary Jackson did not know Eunice Marsden, and had very little in common with her. True, she was married; but so newly married that she still had to shake herself to remember – during the day – that it was true. She was twenty-three, fair-haired, pretty and, in the opinion of all of Charles Jackson's relations, nothing like good enough for him. Still, he'd married and they accepted her – and they had to grant one thing, she showed no signs of wanting to be too extravagant. That was as well, for if Charles had a fault, it was that he was on the "near" side with money. He could have afforded something much better than the tiny, two-roomed mews flat they had, even though it was in a fashionable part of London.

At least, it was central.

It was also charming. Rosemary had unsuspected talents including an eye for *décor,* and by closely studying the more expensive magazines she had carried out the decoration of the flat in a way which charmed everyone who saw it.

"My dear," cooed her only sister-in-law, "you ought to take interior decorating up as a career."

"I *know*," returned Rosemary, sweetly. "I would if I hadn't already *got* a career."

"You *have*, dear?"

"Marriage, darling," said Rosemary, still sweetly.

As her sister-in-law was in the middle thirties, and aggressively unwed, that was unkind. There was in fact much more to Rosemary than many people suspected, and among other assets she had the quality of patience. That was the first time she had scratched back after eighteen months of long-suffering endurance.

She had been married six months now, and was feeling much more sure of herself and absolutely sure that, where most of her in-laws were concerned, Charles took her side.

Charles Jackson was fifteen years older than his Rosemary, a "junior" partner on the legal firm of Merridew, Barker, Kyle and Merridew, and he was expected to have a glowing future. He had recently been Secretary of a Government Committee investigating Drug Addiction in Great Britain – a committee partly of politicians and partly of doctors and pharmaceutical manufacturers. The report, which Jackson had drawn up, was a model of concise reporting; it had helped to make his name.

Secretly, Rosemary believed that he should have studied for the Bar, for he was an excellent speaker, could marshal his facts quickly and had a devastating repartee. She had often heard him in the magistrates' courts, nearly always speaking for the defence of someone who was pathetically in need of help.

There were already those who whispered: "Charles Jackson, defender of lost causes."

Rosemary knew all this.

Rosemary was deeply, tremendously, magnificently happy, and believed that Charles was, too.

Two months after the death of Mrs. Bray, about which Rosemary had read casually in the *Evening Globe,* she had finished what little work needed doing at the flat. It was eleven o'clock and one of the London winter's rare golden mornings, without a trace of fog, rain or snow. One window of the long, narrow living-room overlooked the garden of a large house in the square just round the corner, and the sun was striking the leafless branches of two silver birch trees, and made the bark of the trees look as if they had been coated with luminous paint. A square lawn was immaculate, and two beds of wallflowers were sturdy and dark green.

"I'm going out for a walk," Rosemary decided.

She slipped into a sealskin coat, knowing it would be cold, and in any case it was unthinkable not to wear Charles's main wedding present. As she pinned on a small hat trimmed with the same kind of black fur, she smiled at her reflection and her clear, gay blue eyes, then hurried towards the flight of stairs which led to the front door. Immediately below the flat was the garage – in fact, on the stairs there was a slight smell of petrol.

At the foot of the stairs she heard footsteps outside. The door was of solid wood, without a window, so she had no idea who was coming. Nothing was more embarrassing than having a door opened in one's face when one was about to ring, so she waited.

No one rang.

The letter-box was pushed open, a letter – two letters – came briskly through, and as they dropped, the letter-box clacked shut.

"From Australia," Rosemary said, studying the postage stamp, designed with a kangaroo, on one letter. It was addressed to Charles. "That will be from his friend Masters, Charles will be delighted."

She looked at the other.

The address was typewritten, the postmark was London W.1, and it was addressed to her.

Few letters came addressed to her quite so formally; most of those she received were hand-written. It was dark in the little hall, and she wanted to see the sun again, so she opened the door and went out, still holding the letters. The sun shone brightly on her face, on the cobbles, on the chauffeur polishing a Rolls-Royce on the other side of the mews – a middle-aged man who stopped work for a moment, just for the satisfaction of looking at her.

People did that often.

"Good morning," said Rosemary, and won a ready smile. She slipped the letter from Australia into the pocket of her coat – Charles knew how she loved pockets – and, walking slowly, almost purring in the warmth of the sun, and telling herself that it would be divine in the park, she opened her letter.

It was on plain paper, there was no address and no signature, and there was only one sentence.

*Your husband is unfaithful to you.*

Rosemary stopped moving so suddenly she might have banged against a wall. She stared at the single sentence, as if by doing that she could make it disappear. *Your husband is unfaithful to you*, came so brutally, and the ink was dark and the sentence black, as if already meant for mourning.

Then: "Nonsense!" breathed Rosemary.

She screwed the letter up, but kept it in her hand, and began to walk more quickly, hardly knowing where she was going. First the shock agitated her, and then it made her angry. She clutched the letter more tightly, as if wishing it was the neck of the person who had written it.

"*Despicable nonsense*," she breathed, and quickened her pace still more, until she disappeared from the mews. There the chauffeur, a little puzzled by the way she had behaved, went thoughtfully back to his work.

She had to cross a main road to reach the bus, which would take her to Hyde Park. She didn't cross the road. The typewritten accusation seemed to hover in front of her. Of course it was nonsense, she was a fool even to be upset, it was wicked nonsense, but—

Why had anyone thought it worth sending?

Who could want to make her unhappy?

She crossed the road, after all; twenty minutes later, a little before twelve o'clock, she was in the park. It was really like spring, except that the leaves weren't out, and the branches of the trees against the sky looked like the webs of an army of monstrous spiders. The sun was really warm, and she loosened her coat. A few people were actually sitting on the grass, hundreds were walking, the sounds of traffic seemed a long way off. She went across the fields without thinking where she was going, anxious only to be on her own, asking the same question over and over again.

Why should anyone send such a despicable message?

She looked at the envelope again; there was no mistake, this was intended for Mrs. Charles Jackson.

What would Charles say?

Rosemary began to reason with herself. It was the kind of situation which one sometimes read about but which presented startling problems when it struck right home. Ought she to tell Charles? He was extremely busy at the office, he took his work very much to heart, and she knew that he was preoccupied about a murder case that he was helping to prepare for Old Nod, a leading Queen's Counsellor. In fact, he had come home an hour or so later than usual several nights last week.

She winced.

"No!" she said, in a sharp voice.

One of the grazing sheep, near her although she had not noticed, seemed to hear what she said, and looked up at her.

"It's ludicrous, I shan't show it to him," she said. "I shall take no notice of it."

But she prayed that Charles would not telephone to say that he would be late again tonight.

He did not.

He was light-hearted and natural, had not even brought any work home; the briefing was practically ready, and he was to see Old Nod tomorrow.

Rosemary did not tell him about the letters.

Next morning, while Charles was shaving and Rosemary was getting breakfast, she heard the postman – the morning man gave a sharp *rat-tat*. Usually she left it to Charles to collect the post, but suddenly she felt on edge, and could not wait. There were several letters. Charles Jackson Esq., ... Esq. ... Esq. ... *Mrs. Charles Jackson.*

It was almost the same envelope, might have been the very one, had she not screwed it up. She stared at it, and turned towards the door, her lips set very tightly and her jaws hurting because she was gritting her teeth so much. She moved slowly. She could hear the bacon sizzling, but it no longer seemed to matter. Half-way up the stairs she put the letter down the neck of her dress, and then dropped one which she hadn't seen before, and which had been immediately beneath the hateful one.

*Charles Jackson Esq.*

But this was very different.

This was a small, pale-blue envelope, the handwriting was rounded and feminine, and there was a faint perfume. Nothing like this had ever come here before. She reached the top of the stairs, and Charles called out: "Two minutes, pet!"

"All right!" She hurried up.

He was bustling this morning, quite hopelessly preoccupied with a coming briefing session with Old Nod – it was his first direct encounter with the great man. He put the letters on the table by his place, and hurried to eat his breakfast. He was obviously surprised that it wasn't ready, and Rosemary sensed that he would easily fuss this morning. Normally she would have fooled with him, but she wasn't in any mood for fooling; the corner of the letter poked into her breast.

"I won't be a jiffy," she said, "you go and look at your post."

"Oh, no," he said, "I'm not thinking about anything else until Old Nod's blasted me out of his chambers. 'The secret of success', as our Mr. Merridew Senior so often says, 'is concentration, my boy, concentration. When you have any matter of extreme importance, give it *all* your attention, don't dissipate thought or energy. *Concentrate.*'" He was a good mimic, and Rosemary laughed in spite of herself – and in spite of the fact that he had thrust all the letters into his pocket, including the scented one, which could so easily be a *billet doux*.

The coming session didn't impair his appetite. He kissed her as firmly as usual. One moment she was afraid that he was going to notice her letter, but he didn't seem to – and he hurried downstairs and waved back from the front door, then went hurrying out, a rather slim man, slightly above medium height, wearing a black coat and striped grey trousers and a bowler, and carrying a black briefcase.

She took out her letter.

*If you don't believe it, search the pockets of his light-grey suit.*

At first she told herself that she would do nothing of the kind, but would wait until Charles came home tonight, and show him both the letters. Within five minutes, her resolve weakened. She went into the bedroom. There was only just room for the double bed, the dressing-table and few oddments of light-oak furniture; the big wardrobe was built into the wall. She pushed the sliding doors open vigorously, knowing exactly where to find Charles's light-grey suit.

There it hung.

She touched the hanger, but didn't take the suit off the rail. She felt mean and sneaky, as when at school she had sometimes felt mean and sneaky; and she hesitated for a long time. Then, she said in a clear voice: "I won't be able to rest until I've looked."

She took the suit off the hanger, and carried it into the big room, in front of the window, still reluctant to feel inside the pockets. It was well pressed, she'd actually hung it up for him after he had last worn it, and checked that it didn't need pressing. He was very neat with his clothes, almost a dandy.

She held the coat up, and began to go through the pockets, with her lips set tightly and her eyes narrowed as she watched her fingers, as if condemning them for an act of treachery. The first thing she discovered was the last she expected; a faint perfume, immediately recognisable as the same as the perfume on the letter. It came from inside one of the jacket pockets as the lining rucked up a little; the perfume was noticeable on her fingers, too.

There were also traces of powder on her fingers, and none of her compacts leaked; not that she ever asked Charles to carry a compact for her.

His pale-grey silk handkerchief was still neatly arranged in the breast pocket. She took it out. A smear of lipstick showed up quite unmistakably, and there were other smears, probably of lipstick which had been rubbed off – his lips, his cheek, his forehead, anywhere.

Now she had to make a desperate decision; to confront him with this, or to wait.

Roger West knew nothing at all about this, at the time. Yet he was implicated, indirectly, for he had been in charge of the investigation into the murder of an old lady whose nephew now stood arraigned, and whose trial was due next week at the Old Bailey, with Old Nod leading for the defence. It was not one of the Yard's strongest cases, and the Assistant Commissioner, the Public Prosecutor and Roger West were of one mind about it. None had any doubt that the nephew was guilty, but there were serious weaknesses in the chain of evidence against him; properly exploited, those weaknesses could get him off. Old Nod had a genius for finding weaknesses even where there was none, and when he had learned who was to lead the defence, Roger had groaned.

He knew the firm of *Merridew, Barker, Kyle and Merridew*, and had been in the Magistrates' Court on a number of occasions when Charles Jackson had appeared for some defendant or other, usually on trivial charges. Jackson was one of the few solicitors who stood out in preparing a case, and it was already evident that he much preferred working for the defence than the prosecution.

"He's going to give us a lot of trouble," Roger prophesied to the Assistant Commissioner that morning. "When this job's over I'd like to meet him, try to find out what makes him tick."

"You mean whether he's just a clever beggar, or whether he's a man with a mission," the A.C. said dryly. "Don't know which type I like least. Never mind what drives him, you try to block up those holes in our case, I don't want that nephew to get off."

This third crime, then, began quietly and poisonously, and in the beginning Rosemary Jackson did not really understand that it was a crime, and also part of a pattern. All she knew was that until the first letter had arrived she had been unbelievably happy; now it was difficult to be normal when Charles came home in the evening. She didn't know how she was going to face him without telling him about the letters, but if they were wrong, if – even if – the evidence she had found could be proved false, she would have disturbed and upset him at a time when it was essential for him to concentrate.

The fourth crime was very different from any of the others, except in one way.

It was violent.

It also concerned a woman, a middle-aged, aggressive, married woman, a great do-gooder in the north London suburb where she lived, with a pungent tongue and a reputed fearlessness in expressing her opinions from the Bench. For she was Chairman of the Justices at Ligate, and a powerful woman, too.

On the night of the crime she was alone in her house overlooking a heath, completely unafraid and unsuspecting.

## Chapter Three

## The Third Crime

The man approached the magistrate's house by the gateway which led to the garage and the back. It was a dark entrance, for the nearest street-lamp was a hundred yards away, no other houses were near on this side, and no lights showed at the back of the house, although some blazed out at the front.

The unseen man moved stealthily towards the back door and the back windows, making very little sound. He wore dark clothes. It was nearly the end of March, and near the end of the moon's phase. There was a high wind and scudding clouds, with stars glowing here and there, only to be hidden swiftly. The man tried the back door, and found it locked – as he had expected – and then, using a torch very cautiously, he also examined the windows. All the catches were fastened, and he made no attempt to force any one. Instead, he stood back and looked up at the first floor, and could just make out a sash-cord window open a little at the top.

There was no sound but the wind.

Above the doorway was a small porch.

It was not difficult to reach up, grip the top of the porch and hoist himself upwards. His feet dangled and scratched against the brickwork, and by the time he reached the roof of the porch he was gasping for breath, but soon he knelt there quite safely, grinning as he gasped. He waited until he had recovered his breath, then stood up and found that he could reach the open window without difficulty; there was no danger of falling off unless he was very careless. He leaned a little towards the right, and pushed the window down; it moved easily. There was no light here, only greyness and strange shapes, the wind and the winning trees. He edged towards the window, until he was close enough to climb through.

A car turned into the road, its headlights casting a great pale glow.

The man on the porch seemed to freeze.

The lights swayed up and down, the engine roared, and then the car reached the corner, the driver braked and swung towards the heath, travelling much faster than he should by night, even on empty roads; he was doing fifty, at least.

Before the glow of the headlights vanished, the man was inside the house, and standing in a wide passage. On one side was the blank wall and the one window, on the other were three doors. He walked past these, and found himself at a wide landing. Light shimmering from a huge chandelier spread about the landing and the passages, and lit up the wide staircase and the big hall, with its panels, its fading portraits and its evidences of family pride. Once there had been money here; now there was courage and tradition and determination not to allow the past to rot.

In short, there was Councillor Mrs. Jonathan Edward Kitt, O.B.E., J.P., at this moment in the smallest of the four rooms on the ground floor.

She sat with her back to the door, at a writing-desk which had been made by craftsmen three hundred years ago, studying some papers and occasionally making notes. The light from an open fire shone on to her right side, giving her leathery cheek a reddish tinge and putting a fiery glow into her eyes. On the other side there was light from an anglepoise lamp, bright on her grey hair and – on that side – silvery face, on her full neck and on her strong hands. She wore a suit, but it was warm in the room, and the coat was draped over a corner of the chair. Her blouse was much too frilly for a woman of her size, a delicate bluey-mauve thing, trimmed with a lot of lace. Mrs. Kitt liked lace and frills as personal adornment, in a kind of aggressive defence against her plainness and her masculine strength.

Certainly she looked much more like a man, from the door, than like a woman.

She breathed wheezily.

Nothing distracted her attention, she heard no sound outside, and did not hear the handle of the door turn. Papers rustled as she worked. A car passed outside, the second in ten minutes, but she hardly heard it.

The door opened, very slowly.

Then, sharp and harsh and alarming, a bell rang. It startled the intruder, but he had the sense not to slam the door. It made Mrs. Kitt start, but that was all. She didn't put her pencil down and didn't stop reading the papers, but stretched out her left hand for the telephone, and announced in a hoarse voice: "Mrs. Kitt speaking.

"Who? ...

"Oh, Councillor Willerby, I've been hoping you would call." That sounded something like a pronouncement of doom, and at last she forsook pencil and papers, and concentrated massively on the caller. "Eh? ... Yes, of course I've studied it, I'm studying it more closely now, and I am not at all satisfied that we should spend the taxpayers' money so freely ... I know very well that it won't cost much per head of population, give me a *little* credit for thinking occasionally, please ... The simple fact is that it's extra money, it would cost a tuppenny rate, and I'm not at all sure that I can give the project my support ... No, I haven't finally made up my mind, I agree that we must do something drastic about this car parking, the way this country persecutes the motorist is positively dreadful, but that is beside the point. Is *this* the right way?"

She listened wheezily.

The man at the door had opened it just wide enough to slip into the room. Watching her tensely, he closed the door. Then he took a length of chain from his pocket, a piece of bicycle chain, about a foot long, which dangled down; there was ample wrap round his gloved right hand. His reflection showed in a mirror over the fireplace, but he did not notice that; he watched the back of Mrs. Kitt's head, the wiry grey hair braided and coiled just above each ear, the hair at the crown pulled tight, making it very thin.

The man drew within arm's reach of her.

"*Cou*ncillor Willerby," grated Mrs. Kitt in her most aggressive council-chamber voice, "I am well aware of my duty to my fellow man. I am equally well aware – have I not often declared it from the Bench – that in my opinion the motorist is the victim of nearly every ramp known in the civilised world. He is taxed on his car, his petrol, his tyres, his oil, on everything. He pays an outrageous price for every kind of service, unless he is very lucky. He is continually harassed, even *hounded*, by the police, he can never find room to put his car at a convenient place, but that does not mean that I can support any measure which would assist him at the expense of other members of the community, certainly not the *Li*gate Community."

She was wheezing very heavily when she finished.

Then, abruptly: "Very well. If you can't be civil about it, there is no need to discuss it further. When I promised you support for a plan for parking in the borough, I assumed that it would bear some relation to the practical difficulties of the situation. Good—"

There was a sharp sound in her ear, as Councillor Willerby rang off.

She didn't speak, but put the receiver down slowly, and then pressed one hand against her forehead. The man behind her could not see her face, and therefore did not know that she had closed her eyes, as if suddenly she felt very, very tired. Slowly, she bowed her head, and could not have placed herself in a better position for the first blow.

"What is the matter with me?" she asked, of herself and the room she believed to be empty. "He's a civil enough little man, why must I—?"

She broke off.

She heard a sound behind her, and tried to twist round in her chair, but she could not. She heard another sound; the clink of metal. Out of the corner of her eyes she caught sight of the man, but she could not see his face; all she really saw was dark-grey serge and bright, shiny black buttons.

Then, savagely, he struck her.

She cried out, in terror and in pain.

He struck, and he struck, and he struck her again.

He went out, nearly twenty minutes later, leaving her lying by the chair, from which she had fallen, with blood on the carpet and on her hands and arms where she had tried to protect herself. It was difficult to be sure whether she was breathing or not; in fact, she was.

Her assailant went out by the front door, and then hurried across the overlong grass towards the side entrance. He stepped out, keeping close to the high wall and the hedge behind it, and even had anyone been there, he would have been difficult to see in the darkness.

He reached a corner.

A cyclist was coming round another distant corner, between him and his small, parked car. As he drew nearer and the cyclist approached, he saw that it was a policeman. He heard the sound of the tyres on the road. There was a chink, as of metal, and a faint ring of the cyclist's bell, caused by vibration.

The policeman passed.

The man in dark grey took no notice of him, but went to his little car, the lights of which glowed dutifully, and got in. Then he looked round, but the policeman had turned the corner, and the wide road was empty again.

The driver started the engine, and soon the car moved off.

## Chapter Four

# Roger West

Chief Inspector Roger (Handsome) West of New Scotland Yard turned into his office, the morning after the attack on Councillor Mrs. Kitt, and was surprised to see the four Chief Inspectors with whom he shared the office grouped together near a window. These were men whom he knew so well that they were easily taken for granted. There was Eddie Day, with his enormous paunch, and with protruding teeth which prevented his mouth from closing completely. There was massive and tall Bill Sloan, recently back from one of the Divisions, fresh-faced and fair-haired and looking more like a professional footballer than a professional detective. There was Calder, plump, plaintive, shrewd. And there was Jim Reedon, smallest, shortest and oldest of the group.

"Hallo, Roger, you heard?" Reedon asked at once.

"Public holiday, or just a holiday for crime?" asked Roger. A huddle like this meant something unusual, and something which affected life at the Yard – such as a rumour of a new bonus or new night schedules, or posting for seniority. As soon as he spoke, he realised that he had misjudged the mood of the others, and added more soberly: "No, I've only just got in."

He had a strange impression: that they weren't certain how he would take the news they had to give. Even Sloan, his oldest friend here, a man who had worked under him for years, gave the impression of being ill-at-ease. Reedon obviously didn't like what he had to say; his dark-brown eyes were very expressive.

"Is it the Newman appeal?" Roger demanded. "They haven't granted—"

"It's the A.C.," said Reedon, "coronary thrombosis last night, and it's touch and go."

"Oh," said Roger, sharply. "Oh." He understood their mood, now. Slowly he put his right hand to his pocket and drew out cigarettes. He lit one, watching the others intently, knowing exactly why they had disliked the task of telling him. He drew the tobacco deeply down, and then said, "Where is he?" But it was only for the sake of something to say, because it made no difference where Sir Guy Chatworth, the Assistant Commissioner for Crime, was lying close to death.

"Westminster Hospital," Reedon said.

"When was the latest news?"

"Just had it from Cortland, and he'd just had it from the Secretary," Reedon told him.

"Oh." Roger drew at the cigarette again.

He had been drawn into the group and was one of them and yet in a way apart from them. He could look out of this window into the big courtyard below or across at the countless windows in the other wing of the Criminal Investigation Department building, and find it easy to imagine Chatworth at any of them. The big, burly man, second only to Eddie Day in girth, with the healthy weatherbeaten cheeks and the bright-blue eyes, the fringe – almost a halo – of grizzled hair, and the big bald patch which gleamed like polished teak. That was Chatworth, the man who looked like a farmer, who could be irascible, who could be downright bloody-minded, but was by far the most popular Assistant Commissioner Roger had known in the Department.

"Every copper's friend," a cynic had once said, and been very near the mark.

Roger West's friend.

There wasn't a man in the Department who would not take it for granted, and rightly, that this news would affect Roger more than it would affect any other individual. Chatworth and he "saw" problems in much the same way. Only yesterday evening they had been talking together in this room, when Chatworth had looked in to tell Roger that he'd still not heard from the Court of Criminal Appeal about a convicted murderer's last bid for his freedom. The murderer, Newman, was the young man who had been convicted of murdering his aunt, a touch-and-go case which Chatworth and Roger had worked on for weeks.

"The Secretary's going to send bulletins round as they come in," Reedon went on.

In other words, there was nothing at all for Roger to do. That hardly needed saying. He took the cigarette out of his mouth and tossed it, half-smoked, into the dull little fire in the big fireplace. A few lumps of coal glowed red. Outside, the courtyard was very bright, for it was a sunny morning at the end of March.

"Cortland wants a word with you when you've looked through the things on your desk," said Reedon.

"Thanks. What kind of a night was it, generally?" Roger moved towards his own desk, in the corner farthest from the door. It was a bright yellow, with trays at the back marked *In, Out, Pending* and *Finished*, and with a swivel chair behind it. There was a dark mark on the wall, where the back of the chair continually banged when Roger got up or sat down.

"So-so." That was Bill Sloan, whose desk was alongside Roger's. The others broke up, too, very little time was ever wasted in this room. "Nasty job out at Ligate. I think that's what Cortland wants you for."

Roger said: "Nasty, eh?" and sat down.

It wouldn't have been so bad but for the rider which had been added to the news: that it was touch and go with Chatworth. That was the hard thing to take. It wouldn't have been so bad if Chatworth hadn't been in here late last evening, with everyone else gone, talking about the Court of Appeal. But however bad it was, there was the day's work to face, the old cases to work on, a few to finish off, a few to start. The papers on Roger's desk were fewer than usual, as it happened; in the past few days he had been able to put several files in the *Finished* tray, and they were now matters of memory and *Records*.

He looked through the pending cases, made a few notes, put two files aside because he wanted to discuss the cases with one of the Superintendents, and then found himself with a copy of a report from HA Division – Ligate. It was a good report, containing few wasted words. An elderly and distinguished citizen of Ligate had been brutally attacked in her home near Ligate Heath some time last evening. She was still unconscious. Robbery appeared to have been the motive, for the room in which she had been sitting had been ransacked. But there were some odd features about the case, and there was a note from Cortland: "See me, will you?" Normally, Cortland would have seen the A.C., and Chatworth would have sent for Roger. Now, Cortland was in the old man's shoes, if only temporarily.

Roger lifted the telephone.

"Superintendent Cortland, please."

"Yes, sir." There was hardly a pause. "You're through."

"Thanks … 'Morning, Frank, West here," Roger greeted. "Yes, I can come right away." He put down the receiver promptly, stubbed out a cigarette, and noticed that it was the third he had finished since sitting at the desk: three in less than half an hour. He got up, holding the Ligate job file. Only Eddie Day was in the office, huddled over some papers at his desk and peering at them through a magnifying-glass. Eddie was the Yard's – perhaps the world's – supreme expert on forgery, and he had a great and almost simple belief in the efficacy of the magnifying-glass method. Nine times out of ten it told him what he wanted, too.

Roger went out.

The news about Chatworth weighed very heavily indeed, and that wasn't a healthy thing. He made himself think of the Ligate job. The one thing he had really fastened on to was the name – Councillor Mrs. Kitt. It was familiar, and he had a feeling that any other morning he would have realised why, by now. Now, it evaded him. Councillor Mrs. Kitt—

*Mrs. Kitt, Justice of the Peace.*

Ah!

The unfamiliar part of the name was "Councillor". Plain Mrs. Kitt, J.P., was a byword. She took the opposite line from most magistrates and justices by stoutly defending motorists whenever she had the least opportunity. Sometimes she went very near folly in her defence of them. It was easy to recall some of her pet outbursts, often quoted in the London evening newspapers, occasionally reaching the heights of the morning dailies.

"There are times when it appears to me that the average policeman has nothing better to do than to lurk in dark corners so as to pounce upon an unsuspecting motorist who has parked his car in the wrong place," she would say, and get the headline: *J.P. Says Police Lurk in Corners*. Or she would say: "Why is it that the motorist always gets the blame for accidents? Half of them are caused by the folly of pedestrians or the lunacy of cyclists," and the liberal translation would be: *Cyclists are Lunatics, says J.P.*

She wasn't the only Justice of the Peace with a mind of her own and pungency of phrase, and Roger could not recall any great scandal about her. That implied that she had never gone too far – not far enough, for instance, to warrant the reasoned objections of the local police. The Superintendent at Ligate was old Jem Connolly, only a few years off retirement, and one of the very best. Connolly probably had a sneaking liking for the woman.

Roger tapped at Cortland's door.

"Come in ... Oh, hallo, Handsome." Cortland had once been one of the least-liked men at the Yard, but of recent years he had come out of his shell and become much more respected, although not really liked. Massive, with a pale face and a heavy manner and very little humour, he shared this office with a Chief Inspector who was out of London on a case. "Sit down ... very nasty business about Sir Guy, never been more surprised in my life."

"It shook me, too," Roger said.

"Bet it did. Last man I would have suspected would go down with that."

It shouldn't have been, of course. Chatworth's high colour should have been an indication to all of them. Chatworth's ability to work the clock round should have been another pointer, the excessively energetic man in the sixties was always in line for trouble – no, it wasn't really surprising.

"Anything new in about it?" Roger asked.

"Not to say new. He's in an oxygen tent, getting the best possible attention, that's one thing we needn't worry about. But when anyone gets it as bad as this, they don't often recover. Hell of a do."

Roger said stonily, "Yes."

"Well, this Ligate job," Cortland said at last. "You've got nothing special on your plate at the moment, have you?"

"No."

"How about going over and seeing Jem Connolly?" suggested Cortland. "He was on the phone half an hour ago, says there are one or two things about the attack that he doesn't understand, and he'd like us to send someone over. Trust old Jem not to take too much on himself. You won't need to take anyone else from here, Jem'll put a sergeant at your disposal. Anyone else you want, too, unless you'd like to take someone from here?"

"Shouldn't think there's any need," Roger said, "HA Division's pretty good."

"That's what I thought. Okay, you get going, and I'll call Jem and tell him you're on the way."

"Fine," said Roger. "Thanks."

He had a shrewd suspicion that Cortland had assigned him to the Ligate job because it would give him plenty to think about when he wouldn't want time on his hands, or even time in which to go painstakingly over all the pending and unsolved crimes that needed attention.

It would be good to get his teeth into something tough.

As he went back to the office, Roger made a mental note of the things he ought to put in hand before he left for Ligate, where he would probably be for the rest of the day. One thing, his wife was away. He'd have two or three telephone calls made, and call Charles Jackson; he'd made a tentative luncheon date with the solicitor whose preparation of the case for the defence of young Newman had come so near success.

Eddie Day, still at the office, glanced up myopically, and then turned back to a cheque pinned to a sheet of white paper on his desk.

The operator made notes of what Roger wanted her to do, and then said: "I'll get Mr. Jackson for you now, sir."

"Thanks."

He had come across Jackson more often than many solicitors, and liked what he knew of him; Chatworth had once agreed that Jackson might possibly be a man with a mission. In the past few weeks, however, Roger had sensed a change in the lawyer's mood. It was almost as if Jackson was losing his confidence – conceivably the big effort in the Newman job had taken some of the vitality out of him.

"You're through to Mr. Jackson, sir."

"Hallo, Mr. Jackson," Roger said, "this is West of the Yard. Good morning."

"Good morning," Jackson said. He wasn't brisk or eager or in any way self-assertive; rather, he was flat.

"I'm really sorry, but I've been detailed to a job out at Ligate, and I don't think there'll be any chance to get back to town for lunch," Roger said. "May I call you as soon as I know when I have a free date?"

"Oh, *damn*," Jackson said roundly and quite unexpectedly.

"I'm sorry if I've—"

"No, don't take that personally," said Jackson, with more vigour in his voice, "but I particularly wanted a word with you, on a—well, on a private matter. I thought we might manage it at luncheon. Look here, can you spare me an hour this evening? Or some time, soon?"

He was really anxious; there was no doubt about that.

"This evening will do fine," said Roger. "Would you care to come round to my place for an hour after dinner? Eight-thirty, say?"

"That's very good of you, Mr. West, and I would. You won't mind me—" Jackson broke off, as if he wished he hadn't started to say that, and then went on more abruptly: "That can keep. Eight-thirty, then, at Bell Street."

"I'll look forward to seeing you," Roger said.

When he rang off, he reflected that Jackson had taken the trouble to find out where he lived. Well, it wasn't the first time that lawyers had wanted a word in private. It was useless to speculate on reasons, but impossible to disregard the fact that Jackson had been really disappointed about the luncheon, and that his mood appeared to have changed lately.

Roger went to the lift, downstairs, then out into the courtyard, where his green Wolseley was parked. No one spoke to him about it, but he sensed that even the uniformed men there on duty were wondering what "Handsome" West was feeling about the A.C.

He felt like hell.

So, probably, did a lot of other people, including the relations of Councillor Mrs. Kitt, J.P. He wondered whether she had recovered consciousness, or whether she would die and so make this another murder.

He would soon know.

## Chapter Five

## The Observant Policeman

"Here's the room," said Jem Connolly. "I didn't have anything taken away until you came, never know what you geniuses at the Yard will want. Go in proper fear and trembling of you, we do."

"So you should," said Roger, straight-faced.

With his matter-of-fact-ness and rather heavy-handed humour and sarcasm, Connolly had done him good. He was an unlikely looking man to be a senior Divisional officer, and shorter than most; he could only just have squeezed into the regulation height when he had first joined the Force over forty years ago. The years had withered him and bowed his shoulders, and now he was positively small. Roger stood a head taller, at just over six feet, massive and brisk-moving. A shaft of sunlight coming through the open front door of the house near the Heath shone on his short, wavy fair hair.

Several Divisional men were outside, and more of them in here. The main jobs had been done – the measuring, the photographing, the testing for fingerprints, the searching for clues. Outside, the house was of ugly, late Victorian design, with red brick walls and a spiky turret with a tall, slated roof, rather like a steeple. Inside, the hall and the rooms were large and well proportioned, and although the first impression was one of shabbiness, the general effect was imposing.

Connolly led the way into a room on the right, not large, yet larger than any in Roger's Chelsea home. Now the size of the room hardly seemed to matter, only its chaotic state. Papers had been torn up and scattered over the floor, and there was a heap of burned paper in the fireplace – black, crinkly and shiny, and showing clearly that much of it had been newsprint. A large glazed mahogany bookcase, set against one wall, stood wide open, and most of the papers appeared to have been taken from the bottom of the bookcase, which formed a shallow cupboard. Two or three large books had been ripped to pieces until only the leather binding was left.

"Don't tell me," Connolly said, "he was looking for something."

"Who's he?"

"Don't you run away with the idea that a woman did this job, Handsome."

"I just like to know," said Roger, dryly. "Any photographs ready, Jem?"

"Coming by special messenger."

"Thanks."

Chatworth was forgotten, as everything was forgotten in the task ahead. Here was an almost perfect crime for demonstration purposes – the littered room, the torn books, the burnt papers, the open cupboards and drawers – and, on the floor just in front of a writing-bureau and by the side of a chair, the chalked outline of the figure of a woman. Roger studied it.

"So she's big."

"Five feet eleven, fourteen stone and more."

"How is she?"

"Still unconscious."

"Chances?"

"They won't say. Her husband's at her bedside," said Connolly.

"Where was he last night?"

"Out at a meeting. They're the most persistent do-gooders in Ligate. Between you and me, Handsome," Connolly went on earnestly, "I like the pair, and I think I prefer old Dr. Kitt to his wife. Not much, though; she's always shooting her mouth off about the police persecuting motorists, but she's got more milk of human kindness in her little finger than a lot of people have in their—well, never mind. She makes a lot of noise, but does a hell of a lot of good. She's behind nearly all the youth-club movements in the borough, the old people's homes, the sick visiting, the—well, Mrs. Kitt and Social Welfare are synonymous terms round this part of the world, no one worries about her letting off steam about parking regulations. Truth is, she's sour about parking laws," Connolly went on, with a twinkle in tired grey eyes. "She drives a big old Austin, and can't park for nuts."

Roger was studying the bureau.

Standing on it was a framed photograph of a youngish woman – with a fresh, attractive face, a look of humour and intelligence; the kind of photograph one would automatically look at twice.

"Who's that?" he asked.

"Mrs. Kitt's niece – her only near relation," Connolly told him. "Name of Akers – June Akers."

"Wonder the chap didn't smash that up," Roger observed. "What meeting was Dr. Kitt at?"

"The local Town Hall; there's a protest campaign going on about pulling down a row of old houses on the other side of the Heath. Insanitary and useless, anyhow, but the landlords and the tenants are squealing. Dr. Kitt was chairman of the meeting, which lasted from eight o'clock until eleven, and went on with some friends for a cup of coffee. His wife was found about ten-thirty."

"How?"

"I train my coppers."

Roger grinned. He was paying attention and looking about him at the same time. The books, some of them open on the bureau, had not been damaged – but close to the wall there was a heap of old newspapers, some standing up like a newspaper tent. It looked as if the attacker had been prepared to destroy them all, but had stopped with the job half done. Some of the newspapers had been torn into small pieces, and now Roger saw that the big book covers, with the insides torn out, had been press-cutting books.

"... and this particular copper, name of Pye, smelt burning, and decided he ought to come and have a look," Connolly was saying. "He said he thought it was a chimney fire, but a few bits of charred paper fell on him as he was cycling along, and he wanted to make sure. He looked through a gap in the curtains"—Connolly pointed—"and saw her."

"Any idea how long it was since she'd been attacked?"

"Yes, I think so," said Connolly. "There's a Councillor Willerby ready to swear that he talked to her on the telephone at nine-five – in fact, for nearly twenty minutes until nine-five. They had a bit of an argument over some Council bother, and talked so long that she prevented him from hearing the beginning of the news. He's a Home Service fan, and likes to hear Big Ben every night. What with Mrs. Kitt's objection to a parking scheme Willerby was putting up, and keeping him late, he was in a pretty foul temper. But he lives on the other side of the Heath, and his wife and five children can testify that he didn't go out."

"What's the parking scheme like?"

"All Ligate needs is about twenty-five philanthropic millionaires, and we might be able to afford it. The truth is, Handsome, Mrs. Kitt had her head screwed on the right way, she didn't go wrong very often."

"Really fond of her, eh?" Roger said, smiling.

"If she dies, the Ligate Force will work as hard as they would if one of their own chaps had been murdered," said Superintendent Connolly, "that's a fact."

Roger grinned again.

"So will Jem Connolly! Anything much missing, do you know?"

"Twenty pounds or so from a cash box in the bookcase." Connolly pointed to a green-metal box which had been dropped near the fireplace. "It was forced."

"Prints?"

"None found."

"Means of entry?"

"Not sure – could have been from a landing window, or she could have let him in herself."

"Know if anything else is missing – jewels, that kind of thing?"

"They had nothing much of value, they're new poor, and they've sold most of what they inherited to keep going. Yet they're still the biggest subscribers to local charities."

"In short, no known motive."

"In short, no known motive," Connolly agreed. "Thing that puzzled me, of course, was all this – I can understand the chap making a mess of the place if he was looking for money, but why did he go to the trouble of burning newsprint? I can't make any sense out of that yet, can you?"

"None at all," agreed Roger. "You'd better leave that burnt paper to us, Jem. I'll get someone over from the Yard to salvage what he can. All right to use this phone?" When Connolly said, "Yes," Roger dialled Whitehall 1212, and spoke to Cortland, who promised to send a laboratory man and a paper expert over at once.

"Thanks," Roger said. He raked the room with his gaze, and then studied a pencilled sketch of the position of the fallen woman, his head on one side, his thoughts entirely on this problem. "Where was the worst injury?"

Connolly answered very slowly: "That's hard to say. She was badly battered – back of the head, temples, forehead and the upper part of her face. The fellow seems to have gone berserk, but there's one other queer thing. Say—don't you ever make suggestions, or do you wait to be told everything?"

"If she was so badly battered, why is she still alive?" asked Roger, and tapped the medical report. "Most of the injuries are superficial, considerable haemorrhage, but no damage to the skull except, possibly, one crack. That's partly due to the weapon, isn't it? Looks like a bicycle-chain job."

"Right in one," said Connolly. "We could see the marks of the links on her cheeks. He just beat her about the head as if he wanted to savage her, and when she was unconscious, behaved like a madman and did all this."

"Heaven save me from guessing, but someone didn't like her, this wasn't done simply from a robbery point of view. Unless," Roger added hastily, seeing the gleam in Connolly's eyes, "someone came to rob, and wanted to make us think it was personal revenge."

Connolly didn't speak.

"What about the rest of the house?" Roger asked.

"Nothing touched," the Ligate man said, "but let's go and have a look round." He led the way, and they spent twenty minutes in the rest of the house. They stopped at the landing window and studied the marks on the inside and outside paintwork, where Connolly said there were scratches on the tiles and the pillars leading to the porch, suggesting that someone had climbed up; they had found nothing which might be termed a "clue".

"The Kitts have a couple of daily women, one of them an old servant, the other fairly recent," Connolly went on. "I talked to them myself this morning, but couldn't get a thing out of them. Plugged the line that someone must hate Mrs. Kitt to treat her like this, but they say the same thing as her husband, and the husband says the same thing as I do – she hadn't an enemy in the world. So far as we know," added Connolly, dryly. "Going to hunt for secret enemies, Handsome?"

"Let's go back to the room where she was attacked," said Roger, and as they went, continued: "I think I've some bad news for you, Jem."

"You don't have to tell me. Go through those newspaper cuttings, one by one, stick together all those we can. Help your Yard boys to preserve the ash in the grate and find out if there's any clue in that or anything else – we're looking for someone who hates Mrs. Kitt's guts, and it might be someone she's helped to sentence to jail. That right?"

"If you were a few years younger, you'd be good enough to join the Police! Yes. Can do?"

"It'll take some time."

"We could squeeze a bit more help from the Yard."

"Don't exert yourself over there, you've got to keep up appearances," Connolly said almost tartly. He stood surveying the chaos again, then saw a policeman pass the window, and his voice brightened. "There's P.C. Pye, with those photographs. Observant chap, Pye, like to know what you think about him afterwards."

Roger said absently, "Eh?" and bent almost double, to read something in one of the newspapers. It was obvious that in these there were reports of some of Mrs. Kitt's utterances as a Justice of the Peace, and that no one had ever got round to cutting them out and pasting them in books. One sub-headline caught his eyes, and Connolly complained: "I don't believe you heard a word."

"Sorry," said Roger, and picked up the newspaper; it was torn across and across, but this particular item was not damaged. "Ever believe in coincidence, Jem? A couple of months ago a woman was knocked down and killed in a hit-and-run job, but we didn't catch the swine. A Mrs. Bray. And here is Mrs. Kitt pronouncing on the case where Mrs. Bray was a witness, four years earlier."

*Motorist In No Way to Blame,* read the headline, and the story went on: "Dismissing the charge of careless driving against Benjamin Farley Cunliffe, of 77 Park Row, Regent's Park, N.W., the Ligate Justices awarded the accused costs. The accident took place in the Cannon Street, Ligate, in the early morning of May 17th, and Mrs. Evelyn Rawley, aged twenty-seven was seriously injured and is still in hospital.

"Mr. Rawley, chief dispenser at the Ligate Broadway branch of Smarts, the Chemists, would make no statement.

"Later, Mrs. Kitt, J.P., Chairman of the Bench, stated that the driver of the car was in no way to blame; the fault for the accident was entirely that of the unfortunate victim. 'No matter how sorry we may feel for her, we cannot sentimentalise over such facts as these,' Mrs. Kitt went on.

"The Rev. Peter Waite was largely responsible for the agitation which led to the prosecution. Mrs. Rawley was expecting a child in July, and as a result of the accident the child was stillborn.

"Mr. Arthur Rawley, the husband, giving evidence in a high-pitched voice, as if unable to control his distress, stated that his wife had been happily expecting the baby, and had no worries."

"Mrs. Kitt certainly doesn't mince her words," Roger said.

"I distinctly remember telling you about that," said Connolly. "And I also said—"

"That P.C. Pye's here with those photographs, and you'd like to know what I think about him."

"So you do it in your sleep, do you?"

"Only I never have time to sleep," Roger said. "Before we see him – this Reverend Waite. Isn't he Parson Pete?"

"Yes. Moved over Totting way," Connolly said, "and they're welcome. Meant well, of course, but he was always making trouble. The world's full of cranks."

"He just doesn't like the road-accident figures," Roger said dryly. "What happened to this Mrs. Rawley who was injured?"

"Hell of a case," Connolly said. "She was paralysed, and couldn't speak or move. Living death. Finally died about a year after the accident. Not that it made any difference to the court case – she stepped from behind a bus without looking where she was going. If you ask me, pedestrians are as big a menace as drivers."

"We could argue about that," Roger said. "Better have Pye in."

Connolly promptly raised his voice.

"Come in, constable!"

Police Constable Pye was almost a copy-book policeman, and regulation height had no need to be brought down to 5 feet 8 inches for him. He was over six feet full, massive without being fat or looking unwieldy and he had intelligent-looking grey eyes in a rather long face with a wide jaw. He also had an alertness which it would be hard to miss.

"I have the photographs of Mrs. Kitt, sir."

"Thanks." Connolly took them. "This is Chief Inspector West of the Yard."

"Proud to meet you, sir." Pye had a good speaking voice and a direct gaze.

"Glad to see you, Pye. You first discovered what had happened here. I gather."

"Yes sir."

"Let me have the story, will you?"

Pye glanced at his Superintendent. "Yes, sir, if—"

"Repetition won't bore me," said Connolly, "but mind you keep the facts the same."

"Can't alter facts, sir," said Pye, perhaps a little smugly; or else prosily. He looked almost challengingly into Roger's eyes, and for a moment gave the impression that he was going to speak as from the witness box before the magistrate. But he told the story of the smell of smoke and the investigation, and what he had done afterwards, with a welcome economy of words and without any stilted phraseology.

"Very clear, thanks," said Roger. "See that I get a copy of your written report, will you?"

"Certainly, sir."

"Fine. Anything else?"

"Nothing that I'm sure is relevant, sir, just a small point."

"What was it?"

"A little earlier in the evening, on my rounds – I cycle, sir, as there's a lot of ground to cover – I'd seen a man walking from the corner near Mrs. Kitt's house. He got into a car which was parked near me and drove off. I couldn't understand why he should come round the corner to get to his car, there's plenty of room to park almost anywhere. Can't say that I thought it really suspicious at the time, but I noted it. Then when I was on the other side of the house, I got the smell of burning. The wind was carrying to me. I didn't do anything at first, but finished my beat, and then I came back – and this time a few pieces of charred paper fell on me, and I thought I'd better investigate."

"What was the make of the car?" asked Roger.

"A dark Austin Iso, sir, last year's model."

"Sure?"

"Yes, sir."

"Registration number?"

"An unusual one, sir – L573PR." Pye was crisp and precise. "I've never come across a number with the letters broken up like that before, I suppose that's why it stuck in my mind. I've checked – it's a new series, sir."

"Yes. And we'll check that number," Roger said, making a note, "and if everyone on the beat kept his eyes open and trained his memory like you, we'd have an easier time. Thanks, Pye. Did you know Mrs. Kitt?"

"Quite well, sir, yes."

"Like her?"

"A wonderful lady, sir. If she should die—" Pye stopped abruptly. "Is there any further news from the hospital, sir?"

Roger was in touch with two hospitals, half an hour later, and received virtually the same news from each:

No change.

But there was a change – for the worse – in the relationship between Charles and Rosemary Jackson.

## Chapter Six

## Change for the Worse

In the weeks which had passed since Rosemary had first had the anonymous letters, and had found the traces of powder, lipstick and perfume, the situation at the little mews flat had suffered a sharp and painful deterioration. It had begun on the evening of the day of the second letter, when Charles had returned from a wholly successful day with Old Nod, ready for praise and the evening's comfort. Instead, he had found Rosemary quiet and almost aloof, and he had been tired, and soon out of patience.

Their first real quarrel followed, and his chief worry had been that they had not made it up.

Next morning, after breakfast had been prepared, he had left in a chilly silence.

For two days Rosemary had reasoned with herself that there must be some explanation, that the letters couldn't possibly be true. But when she was with Charles she could always see those typewritten sentences, the traces of powder, the lipstick on the handkerchief. On the third evening – a Friday – he had come home to a now familiar reception.

"All right, Rosemary," he had said formally, "if you're going to behave like this, I'll put up with it. But at least give me a reason."

"You know the reason."

"The only reason I know is feminine inconsistency."

She had jumped up, rushed out of the room and, while he had been sitting in his chair, glowering at the open door, she had run back, carrying the handkerchief and the traces of powder. Flabbergasted, he examined them, gradually regained control of himself, and then said in a tone which it was hard to doubt: "I haven't spent an hour alone with another woman since we were married! – unless you call meeting a client in the office, with Miss Tyrwhitt coming in and out, being 'alone'."

"But, Charles, how—"

"I haven't spent an hour alone with another woman since we were married, I tell you. I haven't kissed, hugged, squeezed, necked, seduced or improperly assaulted any woman since—" Suddenly, Charles had given his irresistibly attractive grin, and with his curly hair ruffled a little and his face flushed, he looked not a mature thirty-five, but boyish. There was a long pause, while she stood in front of him, half in tears and half believing. Then he had gone on with a twisted smile: "I began all that kind of thing with you!"

"Charles, if—if you did—how—"

"Darling," he'd said, "we're not in court. I'm telling you that I'm still desperately in love with you and haven't had an unfaithful thought, let alone deed. I remember a scented letter coming from a woman whose son I'd helped in some motoring trouble. But, darling, for God's sake don't try to make me *prove*—"

She'd flung herself at him.

Yet it hadn't been quite the same afterwards.

For one thing, there were more letters, all very brief and to the same point, all on the same typewriter and on the same kind of paper, and all posted in London, W.1.

For another, Charles had to stay at the office several evenings most weeks, over the Newman case. Old Nod was the worst taskmaster in the Temple; so Rosemary was left very much on her own, and it was on the evenings which she was alone that the telephone messages began.

They were very short and direct, and all on the same theme:

"*Where is he tonight?*" the man would ask, or:

*"Don't believe him, he's a skilful liar,"* or:
*"He's laughing at you."*

And these things worked together on Rosemary's nerves, until she was seldom really happy, even in between the bad periods. Although she told Charles about every call, and they talked it over endlessly, at heart she could not trust him completely. She became listless at times, quick-tempered at others. Charles could never be sure of the reception he would get when he got home at night, or got up in the morning. By far the most significant factor was that she became cool towards him, hating herself for it, and yet unable to help herself.

She started to get headaches.

*"We told you so,"* the Jackson family whispered, *"we warned you that she wasn't the woman for our Charles."*

Towards the middle of the afternoon when Roger West was at Ligate, Rosemary Jackson was sitting by the window overlooking the garden of the big house at the corner. It looked beautiful. The early daffodils were up, although not in flower, the wallflowers would soon be blooming, the trees had young leaves, some flowering bushes had responded well to an early spring, and two almond-trees on the lawn were such a shower of delicate pink that it was hard to believe they had been barren and spiky. Yet Rosemary saw very little of this. Her cheeks were pale and her eyes were very bright, as if she had a headache. Logic was useless to her; she knew exactly how she felt, and there seemed nothing that she could do to make herself feel differently. The poison of disbelief in Charles was so virulent that it had defeated her.

She began to dread him coming home. To dread …

The telephone bell rang.

She had begun to dread the telephone bell, too, because it might be "him" with another laconic statement, another reason to believe that Charles was lying to her. She didn't go towards it at first, but when it rang again, she moved and lifted it up as if it were a heavy weight.

"Mrs. Jackson here."

"Good afternoon, Mrs. Jackson, it's Miss Tyrwhitt here. Mr. Jackson would like a word with you."

"Oh." The office. "Thank you."

"Please hold on."

A moment later, Charles came on the line, and spoke with that great care which had become characteristic in the past few weeks.

"Hallo, darling, how are you?"

"I'm all right, Charles."

"That's good. Darling, I'm going to be out for an hour or two tonight."

She felt herself going cold and hostile.

"I see," she said brusquely.

"I wondered if you would care to come with me."

That was completely unexpected, almost bewildering.

"To see—a client, Charles?"

"In a way," said Charles. "To see a man with whom I have a lot of business, and who might be able to help us."

"You mean a *doctor*? No, Charles, I've told you before that I'm not ill, and that if you—"

"Not a doctor," Charles said quietly, "a policeman."

"Are you *crazy*?"

After a moment's pause Charles went on with great deliberation: "I might be, Rosemary, but we must get to the bottom of this business, and I've come to the conclusion that we must ask the police to find out who's sending these letters and making these calls. It's a simple case of poison pen, and in any case—" Charles paused again, drew a deep, hissing breath, and went on: "This is one of the senior officials at Scotland Yard. I know he'll respect our confidence, and I'd much rather you were with me than that I should see him on my own."

When he stopped, there was another pause.

Then: "Charles," Rosemary said, in a catchy voice, "do you seriously mean that you want to go that far to find out who's sending these messages?"

"I've had a private inquiry agent trying to find out, for nearly three weeks," Charles said crisply, "and he hasn't discovered anything. The Yard should do a lot better. Will you come?"

She was nearly crying.

"Yes," she said, "yes, of course I will."

"That's what I wanted to hear," said Charles, quietly. "Listen, darling. Let's have a meal out, I'm not due at this chap's place until eight-thirty. We've plenty of time. I'll be back at half-past six sharp, to pick you up. Be ready."

"I'll be ready!" Rosemary promised fervently.

For half an hour she was breathlessly excited, and even when she began to dress, she felt less harassed than for many weeks. It was a dull, overcast afternoon, and by half-past six it was nearly dark. She was ready with live minutes to spare, looking fresh and lovely and young.

Just before half-past six she went to the bedroom window, to look out towards the entrance to the mews. Charles might come by taxi, although sometimes it was quicker to walk, in the rush hours. She strained her eyes to see anyone coming in the gloom, and saw the little black car parked on the other side of the road without taking any notice of it.

Suddenly she saw Charles, umbrella swinging as he hurried, and she almost cried his name.

Then she saw the car move.

It had its side lights on, but was little more than a dark shape which sprang into motion. The room window was dosed, and she could hear nothing; but she saw Charles step into the roadway, then saw the car gain momentum.

It seemed to leap straight at Charles.

## Chapter Seven

# Hit and Run

Charles Jackson saw the light on at the bedroom window, and thought that he could see Rosemary's head and shoulders. He prayed that it was. During the past few weeks he had come near to despair in a bleak unhappiness which made him doubt whether there was a future with Rosemary, whether his parents and his sister had been right. There had been times when he had almost doubted the evidence of his own eyes – the short typewritten letters, the powder, and the handkerchief with lipstick on. All of this was worsened by the fact that, not many months ago, *Merridew, Barker, Kyle and Merridew* had acted for a man whose wife, wanting to be free, had manufactured evidence against him, and actually started divorce proceedings. Jackson could not, or he would not, believe that Rosemary had the same evil twist in her mind, yet sometimes the way she behaved almost frightened him.

He had used one of the best inquiry agents in London, without results.

He had even had Rosemary followed.

Those occasions when they could discuss the situation calmly had become fewer and fewer; Rosemary was so edgy that any thoughtless word, and sometimes words which were actually quite harmless, would reduce her to tears, or else make her angry. It seemed a long time since he had approached the mews flat with anything like his present eagerness.

Yes, there she was, a dark figure against the light.

If she was as eager as he, then tonight might be the turn in their affairs.

He did just notice the small, dark car, parked on the side of the road rather too near the corner. Normally he would probably have thought that it was too close, but little traffic turned into the mews, and most cars were moving slowly, so that it was not really dangerous. The nearest street-lamp was some distance off, and the branches of a plane-tree in the square needed lopping. The mews themselves were still lit by gas light, in old-fashioned lamps fastened to brackets in the walls. The big garage doors were all dark and closed, the only lighted window was that of his own bedroom.

Now he could see Rosemary waving.

He waved back, and broke into a run.

He heard the car engine, but it did not occur to him that there was any danger. He passed the car, and was about to step on to the cobbles of the mews, when he realised that the engine was roaring. Even that didn't trouble him, and he stepped into the road.

He caught sight of the parking lights of the car out of the corner of his eye. It was swinging round towards him, and was coming fast.

All he could see was the dark shape, the lights and the silhouette of the head and shoulders of the driver, who wore a trilby hat. All he could hear was the roar of the engine. He was directly in the car's path as it swung round the corner, and his only hope was to fling himself forward; if he went back he would be caught on the turn.

He jumped.

He felt something clutch at the back of his coat, and fling him off his feet. He felt little pain, was hardly aware of the actual blow, but lost complete control of himself as he crashed heavily on his forehead.

He lost consciousness, while the roar of the engine filled the mews like an avenging storm.

The car, bumping over the cobbles in a sweep, now faced the man who lay unconscious on the ground; a man completely at the driver's mercy.

Rosemary reached the foot of the stairs before Charles actually fell, for she moved so fast.

She wrenched the front door open and light streamed out into the murk, on to the shiny black of the car which was racing past, on to the pale face. For a split second the driver turned towards her; then he sent the car hurtling forward, a few yards away from the prostrate figure.

"No!" screamed Rosemary. *"No, no, no!"*

She went running.

She could see Charles's right hand flung out towards her as if beseechingly. She saw the top of his head and his body stretched out, and saw the car going towards him as if the driver meant to finish his murderous job.

Then another car appeared at the corner, slowing down.

"Stop!" Rosemary cried. *"Stop!"* she screamed.

She was gasping for breath by then, but knew that it was useless to shout. She had a terrible fear, that there was no hope for Charles. She was wrong. The murderous driver swung his wheel; had he gone straight on and over his victim, he would have crashed into the second car, which was slowing down at the corner. The gap at the exit to the mews was narrowing, as if the driver of the second car meant to block it completely.

Wheels screeched.

The smaller car hurtled out of the mews, with only inches to spare on either side. The driver turned right, and sped towards the next turning; once he reached it, he could take a dozen different roads within a few seconds, and there was no hope of catching him up.

Rosemary was on her knees beside Charles.

"Now take it easy," said the driver who had jumped from the second car, "let me have a look at him, I shouldn't think he's hurt much." Whether they were words spoken simply to reassure, or whether he really thought that, didn't matter; he bent down by Rosemary. As he did so, another car drew up, then three pedestrians arrived, one after the other. There was a mutter of comment.

Did you see anything?

No.

Car was making a hell of a noise, wasn't it?

Think he's badly hurt?

Anyone sent for a doctor?

"Doctor," Rosemary echoed. "Get a doctor!"

"I don't think he needs a doctor," said the man by Charles's side. "The back of his coat's split, probably where the wing caught him, and there's a big bump on his forehead enough to lay him out." He had run his hands up and down Charles's body, then felt his pulse. "In a few minutes he'll probably be able to tell you all about it. Let's get him on to the pavement – I ought to move my car."

"Want any help?" the nearest man asked.

"Is he all right?"

"Hit and run, was it?"

"Damned swine, they ought to be hanged."

Two men raised Charles gently, and as they did so his eyelids began to flutter, and his lips worked, as if he was trying to say something. Soon his eyes were wide open, if dazed, and Rosemary was clutching his hand.

"Darling, are you all right? Darling, don't move, don't—"

"I'm all right," Jackson muttered. "Fantastic thing—he tried to run me down."

"Just get him to bed," said the driver of the second car.

Helped by two men, Jackson was able to walk to the front door, which stood wide open, and one man helped him up the narrow stairs, while Rosemary rushed ahead to put an easy-chair in position for him to sit comfortably, pushed a pouffe up for his legs, and, even before he was in the flat, went to telephone a doctor.

Roger West let himself into his empty house in Bell Street, switched on the hall light, and then closed the door behind him. He tossed his hat on to the peg of a hallstand, ran his fingers through his hair and, frowning, went straight along the passage by the side of the stairs towards the kitchen. There was no smell of cooking, nothing but the quiet of the empty house, which he did not relish at all. His wife and two children were away, his wife looking after a sister who was near the end of nine months waiting for her third child, and the boys were with neighbours who lived close to their school. All this was unavoidable, but it had been going on for a week, and looked as if it might go on for another two or three.

He could go out to a meal, or he could forage for himself in the larder.

He cheered up a little as he reached the kitchen, for a daily woman had been in to wash up everything from last night's supper and this morning's breakfast. He looked in the larder and the refrigerator. She had stocked up, too; here were sausages, eggs, bacon, everything he needed. He'd stay in to supper and strengthen his resolve with a whisky-and-soda. He went into the front room, to pour out, and stood looking round with the glass in his hand. Slowly, his frown returned. This was shabby; there was no other word for it, shabby. Lately, Janet had been talking about new curtains and perhaps a new carpet, but the whole room was *shabby*. Furniture, most of the oddments, curtains and carpets – no amount of polishing and mending could alter that. The fact that it hadn't been used for nearly two weeks left a film of dust, a kind of bloom over everything, and made it look worse than usual.

"It's time we did something about this," he said, aloud. "Money seems to go nowhere at all."

A clock on the mantelpiece – a brass ship's clock which kept excellent time – chimed one, for half-past six. Jackson was coming at half-past eight – be interesting to know what he wanted. That meant that Roger had two hours, and he must remember to keep the kitchen door shut while he was cooking sausages, or the smell would invade the front hall, one of Janet's pet dislikes.

In a corner a canteen of cutlery stood in a walnut stand; nothing would ever make that look shabby, it was probably the best piece they had, next to the piano. Each was a present. The cutlery was Sir Guy Chatworth's wedding present. Roger stared at it, gloomily. There was no fresh news from the hospital. No one at the Yard was really hopeful; in fact, all the reports were bad.

"I'd better tell Janet, before she reads it in the newspapers," Roger mused. He had an understanding that he should call Janet at ten o'clock each night.

He took his whisky-and-soda with him, laid the kitchen-table and started to fry, using only one pan for bacon, eggs and sausages. He cut bread and made toast. For the first few minutes he was preoccupied with Chatworth, but he made himself switch his thoughts to Councillor Mrs. Kitt. That was a peculiar case, with several odd features. Why had the assailant torn up that newspaper, and what had he burned? Why had he injured Mrs. Kitt so savagely, and yet not made sure of killing her?

If he'd used a hammer or a bludgeon, or if he'd strangled her—

Well, he hadn't. He'd used a length of bicycle chain, favourite weapon of a lot of people; two or three small gangs in London had recently been using it to lacerate their victims. The pain of the blows must have been excruciating.

Roger had met Dr. Kitt; a silvery-haired, bewildered man who kept his head very well, but was obviously desperately anxious for his wife.

So far, there had been no clue except the number of the car – a false one. Every policeman in London was on the look-out in case it was seen again, and would report at once. But the fact that it was a false number plate gave the case a different slant. Only hardened, experienced criminals were likely to use false plates.

Why had such a criminal attacked Mrs. Kitt?

Roger watched the sausages jumping spiritedly in their fat, and the eggs popping. The bacon was done too much, and pushed to the side. He wasn't really concentrating, for he was after the motive. "Everyone," Connolly and Dr. Kitt had insisted, "had liked Mrs. Kitt." So far, no one interviewed had suggested that she had any enemies.

Had the motive been simple robbery, and the brutal attack and the wanton damage done simply because the burglar had been disappointed?

Or mad?

Roger dished up. He felt sure he had overlooked nothing, and Connolly was as sound as Divisional men came. Forget it.

He didn't want to forget it.

He was half-way through the meal when the telephone bell rang. The main instrument was in the front room, with an upstairs extension; time and time again he had promised to have an extension put into the kitchen, but had never got round to it. He pushed his chair back, and hurried.

The evening newspaper was in the letter-box; delivery boys were coming later and later. He switched on the light of the shabby room, and picked up the telephone.

"Roger West speaking."

"Hallo, Handsome." It was Connolly, in a voice which seemed to hold a note of jubilation. "Having half a day off, I hear. *I'm* still at the office."

"I've known others who sleep in their office, too," Roger said easily. "What's on?"

"We've found something."

"Chalk it up."

"Might get us somewhere, too," went on Connolly, "but it's startling for most of us who know Mrs. Kitt, and it will shake the old doctor badly. She was being blackmailed."

Roger said slowly: "Oh, was she?"

"Yes. I've just had a call from your Yard know-alls – you'd told them to tell me if you weren't around. The newspaper in the grate seems to have been burned to make a good fire to burn a small book – a kind of diary that Mrs. Kitt kept. Some of the pages have been salvaged and are readable, and your lab boys have managed to read some of the writing on pages that were burnt. It's a record of the blackmailing, nothing less. Telephone calls and anonymous letters – and they've been going on for nearly six months. From what we can gather, the game old dear has been trying to find out who it was. Can you come over, or shall it wait until the morning?"

"I can't come over yet, I've an appointment here at eight-thirty." Roger had no desire to go right across London tonight, anyhow, but the decision could wait. "Did she seem to be getting anywhere?"

"Nothing we've found suggests it. No name's given."

"Any idea what skeleton she had in her cupboard?"

"No."

"Find that out, and we'll probably find the man or woman who's doing it," said Roger dryly. "Was she paying up?"

"Yes. Ten quid a month."

"Hardly a fortune."

"It was, for her – much more than she could afford, anyhow."

"How did she pay?"

"In notes – from some of the salvaged papers it looks as if the fellow saw her most weeks. She uses phrases like 'I've seen him today', or 'I expect I'll hear today'." There was a pause. Then: "I haven't told Dr. Kitt yet," Connolly went on quietly, "wouldn't care to tackle him on it instead of me, would you? I know the old boy so well."

"Yes, I will," said Roger, promptly. "Tonight?"

"I'd rather he had a chance of a night's rest, but if you think it's necessary—"

"I'll see him in the morning," Roger promised, "and I'll get the lab boys to check everything on that burned paper, and get the story right up-to-date. Might explain why the brute knocked her about, of course."

Connolly said: "How do you mean?"

"If she was getting reluctant to pay up, and objected, the blackmailer might have come round to beat her up, so that when she gets better she'll pay rather than have another dose," Roger reasoned. "At least it would give us a possible motive."

"The thing that beats me is that anyone could blackmail Mrs. Kitt," Connolly said, and he sounded really baffled. "I should have thought she had a life as open as a book."

Roger grinned.

"To coin a phrase! Anyhow, this is a crack we might be able to widen."

"Okay, Handsome, you go back to the bosom of your family," Connolly said, " 'Night."

He rang off.

Roger went back to congealed bacon and eggs and cold sausage. He was so preoccupied that he ate mechanically and kept taking a drink from a tankard of light ale which stood by the side of his plate.

He should be used to the fact by now; he *was* used to it – there was simply no end to the unexpected discoveries made about human beings. Those with the irreproachable life and the unblemished reputation so often had some secret vice or some skeleton in the cupboard – oh, he didn't have to learn his multiplication tables!

It was nearly eight when he finished, and he imagined that Charles Jackson would be punctual. It was pointless to speculate on what Jackson wanted – and almost as pointless, in this naive mood, to marvel at the coincidence of finding Mrs. Bray's name in one of the newspapers at Ligate.

There were short notices about Chatworth in the evening newspapers, and big stories about the attack on Mrs. Kitt. The three papers each quoted the figure supposed to have been stolen – one said £35, the next £45, the third £95. Where did newspapers get hold of conflicting figures such as these?

The telephone bell rang again.

"I'll have that damned thing brought in here if it's the last thing I do," Roger said, and went along. "Hallo?" He stared out of the uncurtained window. "Roger West here."

"I'm speaking for Mr. Charles Jackson," a woman said, "I—I am his wife, Inspector." She paused, as if she didn't quite know how to go on, and then went on with a rush: "Would it be possible for *you* to come and see him? He's had an accident and although he could come, he really shouldn't."

"Of course I'll come over right away," Roger said at once. "It'll give me a chance to come out, too. If you'll just give me a note of the address ..."

## Chapter Eight

## Coincidence

Jackson sat in a large easy-chair, his legs up on a pouffe, a whisky-and-soda by his side. He wore a wine-red dressing-gown and slippers, with a cream-coloured open-necked shirt underneath. His eyes looked heavy, there was a raw and painful-looking graze on his nose, and a patch of sticking-plaster over some lint on his forehead. The knuckles of his right hand were badly grazed, too. Otherwise, there seemed nothing the matter with him. His wife, who had opened the door to Roger, was a little excessive in her ministrations and in her anxiety that Jackson should not exert himself, and Jackson seemed to be content to be fussed.

The wife – she was little more than a girl – had fluffy fair hair, one of those incredibly perfect pink-and-white complexions, and china-blue eyes with long, curving lashes. Yet she didn't give the impression of being a dumb blonde. She wore an ice-blue cocktail dress trimmed with dark-blue lace, and wore diamond ear-rings which fitted snugly. Her engagement ring was a solitaire; five hundred pounds' worth at least.

Roger, always sensitive to atmospheres, sensed something here which he didn't understand – a curious relief from tension when one would have expected the reverse.

"Sorry about this," Jackson began, as Roger sat down. "I would have come, but my wife—"

"Obviously did the right thing," Roger said.

Rosemary smiled readily; she had flawless teeth – there weren't many women who had a fragile look of beauty quite like hers.

"He would have needed wild horses to get outside again tonight," she said dryly. "What will you have to drink, Inspector?"

"May I have a whisky-and-soda?"

"Of course."

"And plain 'Mister' is perfectly all right."

She looked at him searchingly, and he wondered again what was in her mind, but she said quietly: "Well, it's easier even if it's not quite such a thrill." She went to a small cocktail cabinet and poured whisky, generously. The room was long and narrow, of blues and golds, and wholly charming. It might be small, but money hadn't been spared in making it habitable.

"How did this accident happen?" Roger asked.

"That's the part you're not going to believe," said Jackson.

"Try me."

"Well, Rosemary keeps trying to tell me that it was intentional, and I thought it was at first, but I suppose the fool of a driver turned a corner and nearly ran me down. He did knock me over." This came out flatly, and Jackson was looking at his wife as if imploring her not to make too much of it.

"Say when," said Rosemary, holding a soda syphon. She squirted until Roger said, "When", then brought the drink across, put it on a small table by Roger's side, and went on in a casual-sounding voice: "As a matter of fact, the driver tried to murder him."

"Now, darling—"

"The driver tried to murder him," Rosemary insisted, and obviously they'd been arguing like this before Roger had arrived, Jackson all for toning the incident down, his wife all for hotting it up. She had a curiously precise way of speaking, and a figure which dawned on one gradually; with a positively tiny waist.

"How was it done?" asked Roger, and picked up his drink. "To his eternal failure, anyhow!"

"I ought to tell you not to take any notice of her," said Jackson, "but that wouldn't be any use. Say your piece, precious, and forget it."

"I certainly shall," said Rosemary, flatly. She had mixed herself a drink, and sat down on a pouffe between the two men, looking at Roger more than at her husband. "I was at the window, Mr. West, and saw everything in perfect detail. The car was parked at the corner, and as soon as Charles came up, the driver started the engine. He drove straight at him. Charles nearly jumped clear, but the car pushed him over and he bumped his head, and fainted. I'm quite sure of that." She stopped, still looking straight into Roger's face, but there was something new in her expression, something which couldn't be faked.

Fear.

"I thought he was going to run straight over him, the second time," she announced. "He drove into the mews, going right round, and the engine was roaring all the time, it couldn't have been in higher than third gear. And the driver drove straight *at* Charles. If the other car hadn't appeared, I'm sure he would have gone over him – he had to swerve away. If it wasn't for that, I'm quite sure Charles would be dead."

Jackson raised his hands.

"She will have it," he said resignedly.

"Of course I will, because it's true." Rosemary sipped her drink. The fear had faded a little, talk eased her tension. "He came into the mews simply to run you down. He was waiting for you. I saw the way he looked as he turned round and drove at you while you were unconscious, and—"

Roger broke in sharply. "Do you say you saw him?"

"Yes."

"Can you describe him?"

"Well," Rosemary began, and hesitated; as if the dumb blonde wasn't so far away, after all. "I think I could, but I'm not sure. His coat collar was turned up and his hat pulled low, and the light in the mews isn't very good, you saw that for yourself as you came in. But he glanced at me, and—well, if ever I saw him like that again, I'd recognise him. He had a little snub nose."

"Evil eyes, too," Jackson said.

"I know you don't take it seriously," Rosemary said, "but I shall convince the Inspector, even if it takes me all night." She turned abruptly to Roger. "Charles simply refuses to take it seriously."

"Of course I do," Jackson said. "Who on earth would want to murder me?"

Roger looked from the solicitor's lean, intelligent face to his wife's. He could sense her stubbornness, and was still aware of an atmosphere which he didn't understand.

"Where do you say this happened?" he asked.

"On the corner."

"Where I drove round?"

"Yes," said Rosemary, jumping up. "I was on the look-out for you, as soon as you turned into the mews I went to the door. I was waiting for Charles, too, looking out of the window, and I know that man turned the corner deliberately, meaning to run him down. If he didn't, why did he start off so suddenly? Why, it was almost a racing start!"

Roger expected Jackson to say jestingly that she wouldn't know a racing start if she heard one. But Jackson kept silent.

"Which side of the road was he parked?" Roger asked.

Rosemary took his arm and led him out of the room, into the bedroom and to the window, after a glimpse of Jackson's rueful expression. He reached the window, with the girl still holding his arm in her eagerness to make her point. She pushed the curtains back, and pointed with her free hand.

"Just over there, d'you see? The car was parked on the right side of the road from here. To knock Charles down, the driver had to rev his engine and then swing round the corner – unless he meant to do it, he must have been crazy. Then he swept right round the mews—"

"Did you see him do that?"

"You're almost as bad as Charles," she said quietly. "No, I was running down the stairs, but when I reached the door he was nearly level with me, and the only way he could have got there was to take a wide sweep inside the mews. I'm positive he meant to run Charles down, but that other car—"

She didn't finish.

Roger turned, and they went back to the other room, to find Jackson lighting a cigarette.

"How much of this did you see?" Roger asked him.

"I didn't have much time to see anything," Jackson admitted, "but I know the car was parked there. An Austin Iso. I heard it start off about the same time as I drew level, and the driver did rev his engine a bit hard. The next thing I knew, it was coming round the corner."

Roger turned his back on the fireplace. Rosemary was no longer holding his arm, but looking at him anxiously, as if she was utterly dependent on his reaction for reassurance. He did not realise what a handsome man he was, particularly in that position and with the light shining on him as it did.

"Jackson, what was the other thing you wanted to talk to me about?" he asked quietly.

It was like dropping a brick on to a piece of glass; and almost possible to hear the smash. Rosemary drew in her breath, Jackson sat more erect, as if he had almost forgotten the other reason, and wished it wasn't necessary to talk about it. His wife moved with that easy grace which made her seem very young, and sat on the arm of his chair. Defensively.

"I don't see how it can have anything to do with this accident, it's something quite different," Jackson said quietly.

Now that the moment had come he found it hard to talk, and instead he started fiddling inside the pocket of his dressing-gown. Rosemary watched him, and waited. He took out a large envelope, and from this shook a number of smaller ones. Doing so, he looked up into Roger's face and began to explain. Once launched, he missed nothing out; and he could quote the messages, written and telephoned, as if he knew all of them off by heart. He told Roger when it had started and exactly what had happened between him and Rosemary, and why he had finally decided to ask for Yard help.

"If we don't get to the bottom of it soon, we'll both go crazy," he said simply.

"Sometimes he thinks I *am* crazy, and that I'm making it all up, or doing it myself to get cause for jealousy," announced Rosemary, very calmly. She turned to her husband, and Roger studied her expression and the look in her eyes; he wasn't at all surprised when she went on almost fiercely, "I love him so much, there isn't a thing I wouldn't do to keep him and to make sure that he's happy."

She put her hand on Jackson's.

It was a tense moment, one when no third party should really have been there. In the girl's eyes there was a touch of radiance, and in the man's a look of adoration.

Slowly, they came back to earth; but such was the power of the moment in them that neither spoke of it, and neither appeared even slightly embarrassed.

"So what we want you to do is find out who's sending the letters, and who wants to pull us apart." Jackson was very matter-of-fact. "You'd better know that none of my family was very happy about the match, they think Rosemary's too fluffy, and—"

"The original dumb blonde," Rosemary put in, "but it's partly my fault, I'm hopelessly self-conscious when I'm with them. No one else affects me that way. Will you help?"

"Of course, we'll have a crack at it right away," Roger promised. He found himself wondering whether this newfound faith in each other was absolute; even whether there was cause for Rosemary's suspicions, in the first place, or else reason for Jackson's fear that she might be "creating" this other woman. Remember Mrs. Kitt and blackmail; remember the countless examples he could cite of people who appeared absolutely normal but in fact had a kink; people who seemed irreproachably honest yet had some vice or had committed some crime. Learn the lesson over and over again – take nothing for granted, not even the simplicity of the love between these two.

"But what?" asked Jackson, dryly.

"You know that it will mean probing pretty deeply," Roger said. "Friends, relations, office."

"If we weren't sure that it was necessary to go the whole way, we wouldn't have brought you in."

"Fine!" Roger sipped his drink, then selected a cigarette from the box by his side. "I'll tell you just as soon as I've any news. I'll need these letters, of course. Have you any of the powder left? The powder found in your pocket, I mean—we need to find who put it there."

"We had the suit cleaned," Jackson said regretfully. "Rosemary—"

"I can tell you what powder it was," Rosemary said quietly. "It was *Nocturne* – Angeli's make it. There was the same perfume on the letter which came to Charles, too."

"Who was that letter from?" asked Roger.

"A Mrs. Kennett," Jackson said. "She dotes on a son who had a nasty accident, and injured a child – I helped to settle the claim out of court, and she wrote a flowery letter of thanks."

"Hmm," said Roger. "Where does she live?"

Jackson gave a short laugh. "At the moment, she's in Cannes – she'll be there for another couple of months."

"Still got the letter?"

"I burnt it," Jackson said, "there was no point in keeping it. But we've got the typewritten letters to Rosemary."

"I'd like to take those," Roger said, "and I'll need a clear description of the man's voice when he telephoned."

"There's only one word, it's husky," Rosemary told him. "Just husky – well, hoarse is perhaps better."

"What I'll do is arrange for one of the Yard engineers to come and fasten a small tape recorder or a dictaphone to the telephone, then all talks will be recorded and we can get a true facsimile of the voice. Unless you get confidential calls here, and would prefer not to have them recorded," Roger added to Jackson.

"I want to find this man," Jackson said.

"You happy about the idea of recordings, Mrs. Jackson?"

"Of course."

"I'll send a man over first thing in the morning," Roger decided. "He'll have a note signed by me, don't let anyone in if he doesn't show it. Now—" He switched the subject briskly, wanting to judge the surprise effect on them of what he was going to say next. "This accident or attempt to run you down. Any attempts on your life, Mrs. Jackson?"

"Good heavens, no!"

"No threats, no form of attempted blackmail, nothing but these letters and phone calls."

"No. No, I mean—nothing else."

Roger switched to Jackson.

"Have you had any earlier troubles?"

"No." Jackson's eyes were rounded, almost comically.

"Good God, man, what on earth makes you think—?"

"I'm not at the stage of thinking anything, I'm trying to find out why this happened tonight," Roger said briskly. "I'm on Mrs. Jackson's side, too. I think it was obviously a deliberate attempt to kill or to maim you, and that's something for all of us to worry about. Have you been threatened?"

"No, I—" began Jackson, then suddenly his voice trailed off. He looked very young, not simply the thin-faced, brisk and competent young lawyer, and for a few seconds he gave the impression that he didn't quite know what to say.

"Darling, *have* you?" Rosemary was alarmed.

"Well, in a way I suppose I have," conceded Jackson, "but so have you, West, if it comes to that. Two or three people I've helped to send down have threatened vengeance, but that kind of thing is common-or-garden; convicted men are always blowing off in dock."

"My records show that you usually act for the defence," Roger said.

"These days I do – and I have for the past three or four years," Jackson agreed, "but I helped to brief for the prosecution often enough when I started. As a matter of fact—"

He broke off.

"He helped to prepare the case against a man who was sentenced to ten years imprisonment, and who was afterwards proved innocent, and pardoned," said Rosemary quietly. "He couldn't bring himself to work for the prosecution after that."

"Hell of a situation if policemen took that line," said Jackson.

"We don't have any choice, whereas you do," Roger said prosily. He didn't comment, but was surprised; he had never heard this about Jackson. The gentleness of compassion rested in surprising places. "How often have you been threatened in the past?"

"Twice."

"And the most recent?"

"Over three years ago. That's what makes it preposterous. I just don't believe—"

"Will you write down the names of the men, and the circumstances?" asked Roger. "Then I can get both checked." He finished his drink and looked at his watch; it was a quarter to ten. "When you've done that, I must go," he said. "I've stayed too long already."

"You must have one for the road," said Rosemary Jackson.

"No, thanks."

"Oh, I insist, you must—"

"If you studied as many accident cases as I do which have followed 'one for the road', you'd probably rule them out, too," Roger said dryly. "It doesn't seem likely, but it's possible that the fellow who nearly killed your husband was drunk. Every other time we pick up a man who's knocked someone over and then driven on, we find that he was too scared to stop and call the police because he'd been drinking, and was afraid of the consequences. Sorry if that sounds like preaching but—"

"It doesn't sound like preaching at all," said Rosemary, in a small voice. "In *theory* it's what I always say, but when you're offering a drink to someone in your own home it seems different. You'd side with Parson Pete, then?"

"Parson—" began Roger, and then chuckled. "Oh, I know what drives him on, but I wouldn't go all the way. Not even a quarter of the way! He's been quiet for some time, hasn't he?"

"As a matter of fact, I had a visit from him only a few weeks ago, when he called a meeting in the district," said Rosemary. "Charles—Charles was working late that night, and I went along. Only about twelve turned up, and he didn't even get the few workers he wanted to form a committee but—well, I rather liked him."

"One of the most likeable men I ever met was a fanatic who believed that, all men being equal, all men's property was really held for the common good," Roger said. "It took us two years to catch him, and we found that he'd sold everything he'd ever stolen and given it to charity. Beware the zealot." He jumped up. "What on earth's the matter with me tonight? I'm talking like a pompous J.P."

"We can stand a lot of talk like it," said Jackson, and handed Roger the note he had been writing. "There's all the details I can give you, but I'll bet it'll be a waste of time." He took his feet off the pouffe, and began to get up slowly; obviously his head ached, but his wife did not attempt to stop him. "By the way, do you know anything about the case out at Ligate? When the woman J.P. was attacked."

"A little. Why?"

"How is she?"

"It's still touch and go, but on the whole I think she'll come round."

"I'm very glad about that," said Jackson, with feeling, "and if you catch the swine who attacked her, I'll take the job of preparing for the prosecution."

"Do you know Mrs. Kitt?"

Jackson grinned. "She was my oracle, until a few years ago. I was articled to Summerbee and Cole, at Ligate, and stayed on as junior for three years, so all my early court work was at the Ligate Court – usually with Mrs. Kitt up. I don't know what it is about her, but she had everyone eating out of her hand, she could make the most outrageous statements and get away with them."

"What years were you there?" inquired Roger.

"Until three and a half years ago – I had eight years in Ligate in all."

"You didn't hear of anyone who took a different view of Mrs. Kitt, did you? Anyone who hated her?"

"No." Jackson laughed, as if it was unthinkable. "That was the astounding thing about Mrs. Kitt, no one ever had a bad word to say of her. Oh, one of the police would swear at her under his breath sometimes; she's an exasperating old battle-axe, but she's so remorselessly upright that you take it all. Righteousness without humbug."

"I know what you mean," said Roger.

On his way home, he found himself thinking less of the Jacksons than of another coincidence which was so startling that he couldn't get his mind off it. In the notice that he had read in Mrs. Kitt's old newspaper, about the case in which Mrs. Bray had given evidence, the driver had been represented in the Coroner's Court by *"Mr. Charles Jackson, of Summerbee and Cole".*

## Chapter Nine

## Hit and Kill

Police Sergeant Arthur Atkinson of the Metropolitan Police was attached to the JK Division, which had its headquarters in Totting. Atkinson was a man in the late thirties who already had seventeen years' service with the Force, and who had every reason to believe that he would soon be out of the uniformed branch and in the Criminal Investigation Department. That had always been his dream. He had made application for transfer several times, and believed that his latest application had the recommendation of his own Divisional Superintendent. He would get a little more money as a Detective Officer, C.I.D., but the money didn't matter all that to Atkinson. He simply fancied himself in plain-clothes.

For the past few weeks, he had been particularly on the alert. If he could find a chance to distinguish himself, it might go a long way towards getting his application accepted, and he did not mean to miss a chance. In actual fact he had not missed a chance in those seventeen years, and his chief drawback was that he had little or no imagination; an ideal uniformed-branch man, but not necessarily right for the C.I.D.

Blissfully unaware of this opinion of most of his superiors, Atkinson was doing his rounds on the night when Charles Jackson had been murderously attacked, and the night after the vicious attack on Councillor Mrs. Kitt. They were extensive rounds, for the area took in Totting Fields, and he had to have a word with every constable on his beat, and make sure that all was well.

He finished one round a little after ten o'clock, returned to the station to report and to get a cup of hot tea, then went out again just before half-past ten. He was a big, heavy man, who rode his bicycle steadily, making no attempt to hurry, and coasting the last hundred yards or so to every point of meeting with a constable.

The first calls were in the built-up area. The tyres of his bicycle purred, and the chain made a slight squeaking sound. It was a fine, crisp night, and the stars were out, but there was no moon. Not far away were the big houses near Totting Fields, some of them very much like the house where Mrs. Kitt had been attacked – but Ligate Heath was ten miles away or more. Most of the lights at windows were out, and soon Atkinson was cycling steadily along a road which seemed to lead to a great void, but in fact led to the fields themselves – actually a large stretch of common land and playing-fields. Beyond the end of this road it was badly lighted; in fact, it was Atkinson's firm belief that the whole of the fields needed lighting much better; as it was, far too many young kids fooled about in the darkness. If he had his way—

He began to think, as he often did, of his eighteen-year-old daughter, Betty.

Betty, Sergeant Atkinson would say, was the apple of his eye, pretty as a picture, sweet as a nut – all the things that a fond and unimaginative parent might well say of his only daughter.

Atkinson turned a corner.

Five minutes later he was due to meet a constable at the next corner, so he was in no hurry. He swung his leg over his bicycle, and began to walk – noticing the small car which was parked a little way ahead of him, with dull rear lights glowing.

Atkinson scowled.

The rear lights were there all right, and so conformed with the law, but they were nothing like bright enough for his liking. Motorists seemed to think it clever to try to beat the law. If it was a bit foggy, and it often was in March, then a cyclist could be on top of this car before he realised it was there; and a motor cyclist would probably crash. But legally the Sergeant hadn't a leg to stand on.

He plodded past the car, then glanced towards the big, dark house outside which it was parked. It was divided into half a dozen small flats, and he knew the occupants; the car – he thought it was an Austin Iso – must belong to a visitor.

An Iso?

Atkinson took a deeper interest, and for the first time for several nights he felt a quiver of hope – that he might have come upon his great opportunity. There had been two requests in from the Yard, pinned up on the station notice-board each asking for information about Austin Iso cars, dark blue or black, of recent design, one with the number L573PR and the other with the number KLK514. The light was so poor that it was difficult to read the number plate until he was within twenty feet of it; and reluctantly he had to admit that the light illuminating the plate just came within legal requirements.

He peered intently.

359 ACO.

Atkinson felt a twinge of disappointment, but had the sense to tell himself that he had been a fool even to think that this might be a wanted car. Austin Iso's weren't exactly two a penny, but there were plenty of them about, and four out of every five would be black or dark blue.

He shone his torch inside, nevertheless.

There was nothing of interest. An old rug, on the back seat, a newspaper folded on the seat next to the driver's, an AA book and what looked like a library book. The upholstery was dark red, and the car obviously well kept.

A little regretfully, Atkinson went on to keep his appointment.

The owner of the car stood watching him, just behind the tall, brick gate-post of the house. As Atkinson went on, the bicycle squeaking a little, the driver slipped out of his hiding-place, went straight to the car, and got in. He made some noise closing the door, but not a great deal, although he saw Atkinson in silhouette against a corner lamp. The sergeant glanced round at him.

The driver started the engine.

It roared.

Sergeant Atkinson heard the door of the car slam, and glanced round almost mechanically. He noticed that the side lights of the Iso were not particularly bright, the whole car give the impression that the battery wanted charging. But its engine started at the first touch of the self-starter, and suddenly it roared.

"*Drivers,*" breathed Atkinson.

He was not at all nervous on the road. For five years he had been on traffic duty, often at the busiest junctions, and he took it for granted that provided he was in the right place and doing the right thing, the motorist would do the same. But the roaring of the engine and the little spurt of sound of the tyres on the road suggested that the car had started off at a crazy speed. He glanced round and at the same time pushed his bicycle a little nearer the kerb.

"God!" he gasped.

He jumped desperately towards the pavement, letting the bicycle go, but he didn't have a chance. The car struck the bicycle and the policeman together. The first blow broke Atkinson's back, and a wheel crushed his skull.

Approaching the corner for his next appointment with the sergeant was a young constable, named Davis, with only six months' service behind him. Davis was a small, pale-faced man – many people marvelled that the Force accepted recruits who looked so small – and he hadn't yet decided whether he liked the Force well enough to stay in it. He was thinking of that as he walked towards his appointment with Atkinson. Atkinson wasn't a bad sort, but he'd been in the Force most of his life, and all he had to show for it was a sergeant's stripes.

"That wouldn't do for me," Davis mused.

He was fifty yards from the corner, and in good time, when he heard a car engine start up. Then it sounded very loud, as if the driver thought it was cold, and was revving it wildly. Some people didn't deserve to own a car, they tore its guts out in a few months.

This engine was certainly going some.

Then he heard a crash.

Immediately he began to run, and by the time he reached the corner he was sprinting. The small, dark car passed the end of the road, its engine roaring less loudly, but travelling at great speed.

Davis snatched out his whistle.

"*Stop!*" he bellowed, and then put the whistle to his lips. It sounded clearly across the fields and along the streets. "*Peeeeeep,*" it shrilled, as Davis reached the corner.

Then, he saw a remarkable thing – a kind he had heard about but had seen only when being instructed in the Divisional Station yard.

The number plates of the car were changing.

Actually no light was on it now, even the rear light was out, but a street-lamp showed Davis everything clearly. The first plate seemed to be lifted out of sight, then another fell into position. He could not read all of it, for it was dirty, but he caught the last two, because he couldn't miss: CO. Then the car's lights went on, and he saw it swinging round a corner, towards a road which ran across the common.

Davis blew another blast on his whistle.

No other car was in sight, and the only sound he could hear was of the engine, fading. He had no choice now, but turned and ran towards Atkinson and the wreck of the bicycle. He saw the sergeant's helmet, standing upright on the kerb, as if it had been placed there carefully when Atkinson had fallen off.

But the sergeant—

Davis had seen Army service in several theatres of "trouble". The sight of blood and serious injury did not greatly affect him, although this shocked him. He saw the way Atkinson's head was crushed, and knew that it was a mere formality to feel his pulse.

That *swine*—

The car was vanishing across the fields, just visible now, and another car came towards it. That other car could have stopped it, but it was a quarter of a mile away, and Davis felt helpless and furiously angry. Why didn't someone come, why did all the people within sound of his whistle stay indoors, why—?

Two men came running from nearby houses, and a third walked briskly from the corner. A car swung round the corner, its headlights on and dipped; a blue sign above it read: *Police*. Questions began to flow, but when men caught sight of that head, they stopped abruptly. Davis gave a despairing look across the common, but the killer car had gone.

One of the men jumped out of the patrol car.

"He hurt?"

"He's dead," Davis said savagely. "An Austin Iso ran him down, and changed its number plates as it made off – dark blue or black, dim lights front and rear, last two letters of the second plate were CO – could possibly have been double O, not numerals. Can you—?"

The driver of the police car was already talking on the radio. More people came hurrying up, and very soon a doctor, too. Before the police could move Sergeant Atkinson, a doctor had to pronounce that life was extinct.

Davis heard the awkward comments of the people who stood helplessly by after coming in response to his whistling. The man from the patrol car was bending over Atkinson, as if he had some desperate hope that he could will the sergeant back to life.

"Wonder what he was after," a man said.

"The sergeant probably caught him red handed, doing—"

"If I were you," Davis said, as that rang a bell in his mind, "I'd check your homes, gentlemen, this man might have been trying to break in somewhere, and the sergeant might have spotted him."

Men began to move.

Then, someone said, in a half-joking manner which made Davis's blood boil: "Better not tell Parson Pete, or he'll hold a meeting on the spot!"

"Save us from that," another man said sardonically.

Davis didn't know much about Parson Pete, except that the fanatical parson lived in the district. It was a standing joke at the Division, although the joke was tempered with a kind of compassion; there was no real malice in comments about the man. Just then,

Davis didn't care a damn about the parson or road accidents. This wasn't an accident, this had been coldblooded murder.

And – there was Mrs. Atkinson, and their daughter, Betty.

"God—damn—that—swine," Davis grated under his breath. "God—damn—him."

That was at half-past twelve.

At half-past two Roger heard the telephone bell, as if in the distance, and with a faculty acquired over the years, was instantly awake. But it was a false wakefulness, because the telephone still sounded a long way off, although in fact it was close to his ear. Eyes still closed but mind working, he stretched out, and as he lifted it he reflected that he was glad Janet wasn't here to be woken up. It was pitch dark; probably very early morning.

"West speaking."

"Is that Chief Inspector West?"

"Speaking."

"Just one moment, sir," a man said. "Superintendent Dalby would like a word with you."

Dalby was on nights at the Yard, and was not a man to call a day-shift officer unless it was really an emergency. Roger hitched himself up on his pillow, switched on the bedside lamp, yawned and waited with the telephone at his ear. He hadn't long to wait.

"That you, Handsome?"

"Yep."

"Very tired?"

"Always on duty. What's up?"

"Job out at Totting," said Dalby, briskly. "One of the Divisional sergeants was run down and killed by a car tonight. The car was an Austin Iso, and a constable saw the number plates changing as it moved off. I've a note that you're interested in an Iso, same colouring, two different number plates – and one of them was wanted for a hit-and-run job, wasn't it?"

"Got the car?" Roger asked abruptly.

"Yes," said Dalby, "it's in a used-car lot at Battersea, I thought you'd like to go and have a look at it."

"Thanks, that's fine," said Roger. "I'll go right away."

Two spotlights had been rigged up at a corner of the used-car lot where the Iso had been found only half an hour before Roger had been telephoned. These lights played on the scene – the car, half a dozen policemen working inside and outside it, scraping samples of paint, of Atkinson's blood, of dirt from the tyres, getting dust collected by vacuum from the inside, testing inside and outside for prints, all of which had been photographed. The policemen worked briskly in the chilly night, while two others stood at the entrance to the car lot, to make sure that no one got in without authority.

Roger pulled up outside, and hurried out. Against the bright light he saw the fat figure of a Totting Inspector whom he knew; Totting bordered this Division.

The constable didn't recognise Roger, but drew back at once when he saw the card.

"Inspector Morgan's expecting you, sir."

"Thanks." Roger left his car with half a dozen others, and walked towards the scene. No one seemed to stop working for a moment, but a man was coming from the office of the parking lot, carrying a big tray with mugs of something hot in them. Roger could see the wispy trails of steam from each mug. He went straight to fat Morgan.

"Oh, hallo, Handsome; Dalby said you'd be along," Morgan greeted. He had a fresh face, two chins and a cheerfulness which wasn't in any way forced. His collar was too large even for his fat neck, because he liked his comfort. "I think we're about through. Got a lot of useful things, including a set of prints as perfect as you could want. With a bit of luck we'll get the brute before long."

"How did you find the car?" asked Roger, as they moved towards it.

"One of my chaps was on the look-out; we'd had a flash earlier," Morgan said. "Very quick job from the word go, this was; someone in Totting ought to get a pat on the back. Anyway, our chap saw this car driven up to the used-car lot, an unusual thing to happen as late as this. He thought it might have been knocked off earlier, to do a job. When he got there he saw that one of the wings was knocked about, a lamp smashed, and some blood and whatnot on the bumper. So *he* didn't lose any time, either. Got something for you, too," Morgan added, as they reached the car. "You bend down. I'm too tired. Rear licence plates," he added, and Roger went down on one knee and then on his side, and saw exactly what he hoped to see.

The number plates were fixed on a swivel system, and could be altered at a touch of a button inside the car. There were three plates:

L573PR
KLK514
359ACO

"So now you've really got something," Morgan said, with satisfaction.

He didn't know how much Roger had, yet.

Roger felt a fierce excitement as he got to his feet and dusted his knee and shoulder down. Earlier, he had seen the degree of coincidence, but this was much more than coincidence. Here was a car near the house of Mrs. Kitt about the time of the attack on her; the car which had nearly killed Charles Jackson; the car which had actually killed this man Atkinson. If they could find the owner of that car they might be able to solve three cases in one go.

There was more.

If the killer-driver had attacked Mrs. Kitt, then Jackson and finally Atkinson, what was the common denominator? What made him want to kill or to injure these three people?

Worse: was Jackson, and was Mrs. Kitt, still in danger?

He had to assume that they were, and would remain so until the killer had been found.

## Chapter Ten

## Talk of the Parson

There was no Chatworth to consult.

There was his big, empty office with the black glass and tubular steel furniture which had been his own choice, but which had always looked out of character for him. There was his secretary, prim in white blouse and black skirt. There was bulky Frank Cortland, the senior Superintendent, taking over at the orders of the Commissioner; but it was rather like being at a wake.

The news about Chatworth was no different, and no one seriously believed that he would survive.

The newspapers had the A.C.'s illness in headlines, this morning, next to the story of the attack on Mrs. Kitt. She had not remained conscious for long, and had not been able to make any kind of statement, but the doctors were more optimistic.

"You've got someone at her bedside, of course," Cortland said, the kind of almost fatuous thing which Chatworth would never have uttered; but Cortland was feeling the strain, too.

"Yes—Jem Connolly's got a policewoman over there."

"Good. What else is there, Handsome?"

"Not much," Roger answered. "I've checked that the woman who wrote to Jackson about her son is on the Riviera and nothing suggests that Jackson's having an *affaire*. That's in, because an Iso car was used. We haven't found any trace of last night's driver, at Totting, or where he usually kept the car," Roger went on, "and the latest reports I've had, from *Fingerprints* and the lab, don't help us at all. Only one set of prints are in the car, and they're not in *Records*. If anything they add to the puzzle – they're the prints of a big hand, whereas the driver of the car is described as small or medium size. I know he could have big hands, but it doesn't help."

Cortland solemnly agreed that it didn't.

"I'm working on the common-factor line," Roger went on, "someone known to Mrs. Kitt, to Charles Jackson and Atkinson, although I could easily cool off Atkinson."

Cortland said: "I see what you mean. If he came along and the wrong number plate was showing on that car, or if he wanted to question the driver for any reason, the man might have decided to run him down. In other words, Atkinson isn't necessarily in the series." Cortland grunted. "What's the association between Mrs. Kitt and Charles Jackson?"

"In court," Roger said, simply. "In his Ligate days Jackson sometimes acted for the local police in the Magistrates' Court. This could be a revenge motive – so now I'm looking for a case where someone thinks he got a raw deal, with Jackson prosecuting and Mrs. Kitt pronouncing judgment. It would probably be someone who chose to be dealt with by the magistrates, not go for trial, and—"

"Years since Jackson prosecuted, though, isn't it?" Cortland didn't miss much.

"Hate can take a long time brewing," Roger said.

"Well, you've got to check, anyway," said Cortland, and tapped the report which Roger had put in earlier in the morning, "Anything yet on these two fellows who've threatened to get their own back on Jackson?"

"No, but there should be some reports in this morning, though. There's one other thing I want to do."

"What's that?"

"Have Jackson and his wife watched, in case this killer has another crack. I'll need four men."

"Take 'em."

"Thanks," said Roger.

He put two men on the task of tailing the solicitor and his wife, and kept two in reserve, to take over a little later in the day. He had the uneasy feeling that the Jacksons were in acute danger, an uneasiness chiefly due to the ruthlessness of the killer. The story was always the same: that dark, innocent-looking car with the dim lights, the fierce revving of the engine and then the merciless attack. Add that to the way Mrs. Kitt had been attacked, and you had the brutal killer, the man who did not necessarily attack in the same way every time, and who might find some other way to strike.

There was more: someone else might be associated with the two victims, someone unknown, someone who might be attacked out of the blue with the same vicious savagery.

It was not just a question of investigation, it was a fight against time, a fight to save lives.

Roger settled a dozen small queries on his desk, after coming back from Cortland, then went along to the lift, and up to the laboratory. That was a repository for many jobs at the Yard which didn't fit into any particular Department; and there was one large, spare room where all kinds of experiments were carried out. Along one wall ran a wide bench, and this morning the bench was literally covered with newspapers whole newspapers at one end, burnt ones in the middle, charred ones at the far end. Against the wall stood burned books and the empty cases of the press-cutting books which had been taken from Mrs. Kitt's room. A camera, on a set of wheels and with a dark cloth over it, stood like a solemn ghost in one corner. Large bowls of chemicals were on another bench, and one man was cautiously dipping charred paper in one of these. Another man was sitting at a small desk in the middle of the room, with some large sheets of paper set out in front of him, and he was correlating everything which was discovered from the salvaged papers. Roger had a look round, and then crossed to this man.

"Found anything?"

"Odds and ends," the answer came promptly; "only one thing that looks as if it might be new."

"What's that?"

"She kept cuttings about Parson Pete."

"Were they burned?"

"Yes, except those which are in the newspapers the chap hadn't got round to – and Mrs. Kitt hadn't got round to cutting out, either. Not that the parson's had much to say lately – either that, or else the Press hasn't been giving him the space he used to get."

"He's writing personal letters to people he thinks might help, and calling meetings," Roger said.

"Reduced to that? Poor beggar!"

"How many cuttings did Mrs. Kitt keep of his?" asked Roger.

The sergeant referred to his list. "We've found him mentioned on seven pieces of charred paper, all newspaper, on three pieces which were burnt at the edges and on seven of the undamaged sheets. It's always the same kind of cutting – when he rants against motorists and criminal drivers. You can imagine she would hate his guts, wouldn't you, not keep press cuttings about him."

"Hmm," said Roger, non-committally. "Where does he live? He was mentioned in a report that came in from Totting this morning – the constable's report, what was the chap's name? Davis, yes, Davis." Roger was almost talking to himself.

"Parson Pete lives out at Totting," the sergeant said promptly, "the address is here somewhere." He rummaged through some newspapers. "Here it is, 188, Fields View. Wasn't Atkinson killed in Fields View?"

"Yes," said Roger.

He checked everything else that had been discovered, but there was nothing new; the men working patiently in the big room might get no more reward for their pains. Routine could be killing, and routine was usually the basis of the Yard's successes. He went down to his desk and called Connolly.

"Hallo, Handsome," the Ligate man said. "I was just going to ring you. The doctors have taken Mrs. Kitt off the danger list, but they say that we can't question her for at least another forty-eight hours." He sounded much more cheerful. "How's Chatworth?"

"No change."

"Oh. Bad."

"Yes. Jem, has Parson Pete ever been active in your part of the world?"

Connolly chuckled, as if Roger had pressed a button.

"He lets off a banger occasionally, yes – he called a protest meeting here about a year ago, just after Mrs. Kitt had let fly at the police for persecuting motorists. The parson managed to get quite an audience, seventy or eighty people turned up, but when he started lambasting Mrs. Kitt they didn't give him much of a hearing. All very good tempered, though, they just laughed him off the platform."

"What about Mrs. Kitt? Was she there?"

"Can't say I remember much about it," said Connolly, "but I have a feeling – here, wait a minute, the Desk Sergeant on duty today was at the meeting, I'll have a word with him." He was off the line for a few moments, and then came back to say: "He's coming up – have a feeling that Dr. Kitt was at the meeting. I can believe he would do anything to make sure that the parson got fair play. Anything new your end?"

"Mrs. K. kept press cuttings of the parson."

"Did she, then? Know him, Handsome?"

"No, I've never met him."

"You ought to, he's worth talking to. Nicest chap possible except when he's on his one subject, but he goes absolutely crazy about that, he'd—half a mo'." There was a pause and a muttering, and then Connolly came back on the line: "Thought I was right. Dr. Kitt was at the parson's meeting, taking notes, and he remonstrated with the people who were kidding Pete. All true to form."

"Find out if Kitt and Mrs. Kitt know the parson personally, will you?"

"Yes. That all?"

"I wouldn't mind a report of that meeting, too."

"Tell you what," said Connolly, "I'll send Pye over to see you, the sergeant tells me he was on duty that night. The sergeant went just to hear what was going on. When would you like him?"

"This afternoon will do."

"Fine," said Connolly.

Roger rang off and sat back, but it was only for a few seconds. He was far too restless. He got up, stretching out for the telephone as he did so. He asked for the Sergeant's room, left word that he was going out to Totting, and, ten minutes later, was driving across Westminster Bridge. Traffic was thick and noisy. Clouds were blowing up, and the effect over the Thames was majestic, with the edge of the clouds rimmed with brilliant gold, and the Houses of Parliament outlined against them. He kept his mind on his job, reached Totting in twenty-five minutes and went straight to the Divisional Headquarters. Nothing fresh had turned up there, no one had yet discovered who had owned the damaged Iso, or where it had been garaged.

The Superintendent on duty had a heavy cold, and didn't seem likely to last out the day at the office.

"Oh, yes, Parson Pete lives in the neighbourhood," he agreed, "don't know that we have as much to do with him as some of the other places. Harmless enough, you know, he's just got the one bee in his bonnet."

"That death by accident on the roads is murder?"

"Thass it," said the Superintendent. "Thass it."

"Mind if I go and have a chat with him?"

"Please yourself, Handsome, but I can't see that it'll do much good."

The parson was an acquaintance of Councillor Mrs. Kitt, and he had called on Rosemary Jackson, Roger remembered; there was one common factor. He schooled himself not to show the sudden surge of excitement he felt as he put the next question, almost sharply: "Did Atkinson know him?"

"You mean, know the parson?" The Superintendent's streaming eyes begged forgiveness for the question. "Can't say I know much about Atkinson, except that he was dull but sound. Would have gone to see the wife and daughter, but with this streamer, well, hardly fair."

"Who did go?"

"Inspector Gale, and young Davis – promising youngster, Davis, did a good job last night. There's the type you want for the plain-clothes branch, Handsome, not Atkinson's type. Poor chap didn't realise it, but he would never have made the grade. I—oh, hell, I'm going to sneeze."

Roger left him, as soon as the bout was over and went downstairs. No one seemed to know whether Atkinson had anything to do with Parson Pete, and no one knew where young Davis was – except that he had been here during the morning, although he wasn't on duty until eight o'clock tonight. Roger left the station with a distinct impression that, with the Superintendent off colour, there was a kind of inertia – a bad Divisional sign.

He had already inquired the way, and drove to the other side of Totting, where Sergeant Atkinson's wife lived. Outside the small, terraced house was a motor cycle, and a smallish, pale-faced man was coming away as he entered the gateway.

Press? Insurance agent? Funeral director?

The man drew back.

"Excuse me, sir, aren't you Chief Inspector West?"

"Yes."

"I'm Police Constable Davis, sir. I—I found Atkinson's body last night. I've just been in to see if there was any way I could help. Hell of a thing to see a family cut up like this, isn't it?"

"Really bad, are they?"

"His missus doesn't stop crying, and that kid – she's only eighteen, but—anything I can do for you, sir?" Davis overcame his feelings.

"I'm after the motive, Davis," Roger said, with a magic touch which made Davis feel as if he was being consulted as an equal. "Last thing I want to do is make it worse for Mrs. Atkinson, but I'd like to try to find out if anyone had a knife in Atkinson – anyone would want him dead. You don't know of anyone, I suppose?"

"No, sir. Man without enemies, I would have said."

"Did you know him well?"

"Well, sir, I've only been on the Force six months, but—well, he did talk to *me*. If you don't mind my saying so, he seemed glad of someone to talk to. He was a bit of an old woman, and the station chaps were used to him. I'm not being critical, I'm being—"

"Factual. Quite right. Was he after anyone around here – anyone he was likely to put inside?"

"I wouldn't say so, sir – bit of wishful thinking, perhaps, that's all."

"Any friends or *bêtes noires*? Like that parson, what's his name, Parson Pete. The parson's always trying to push the police around, and Atkinson was a traffic specialist, wasn't he?"

"Well, he did know the parson," Davis asserted. "He hadn't much time for him, either. He pointed him out to me one night – quite close to the spot where he was murdered, sir, the parson lives near there. Said he was more nuisance than he was worth, that kind of thing. But I don't know of anyone else – and I can't see the parson killing anyone."

"No," agreed Roger, and after a moment's thought, went on: "Davis, do this for me, will you? Find an excuse to see Mrs. Atkinson and her daughter again soon, find out how well they knew this parson, and also if Atkinson knew anything about Councillor Mrs. Kitt when he was over at Ligate."

"Now there's a woman the sergeant would have pole-axed," Davis declared. "What he said about her wouldn't bear repeating to anyone's aunt. I'll certainly do what I can, sir. As a matter of fact, I promised to go back this afternoon."

"Good," said Roger. "Thanks."

He watched Davis straddle his bicycle, and as he did so became aware of a slight movement at the curtain in the window of the Atkinsons' house. He glanced towards it. A girl with jet-black hair and a heart-shaped face was looking out of the window; at Davis, not at him. She did not seem aware that anyone else was outside with Davis.

"Good morning, sir," Davis said, and started the motor vigorously.

Roger got into his car. The girl, presumably Betty Atkinson, was aware of him now, but she glanced at him incuriously, then moved away from the curtain.

Her mother, who couldn't stop crying, the girl standing hopelessly at a window, looking out – was there no end to the pain this case was causing?

Pain.

Someone had wanted to torment Rosemary Jackson, and torment her husband as well – and then had tried to kill. The assailant had beaten Mrs. Kitt with sadistic force. Atkinson had been mowed down, hardly knowing what had struck him, but the trail of pain behind him was as great as that of the others. Who was behind it? Some sadistic monster—

These attacks were cold-blooded, remember.

Roger turned the same corner as Davis had last night, into a long road with two-storeyed, terraced houses on either side, most of the walls of yellow brick, the roofs all of grey slate. A long way off was a bus; nearer, a car was heading this way, and he saw its sign "Police". As he did so, his radio began re crackle, and then came a message:

"Calling Chief Inspector West – calling Chief Inspector West. Please return to Scotland Yard, urgent, please return to Scotland Yard, urgent. Can you hear me?"

Roger flicked over to transmission.

"West speaking – can you hear me?"

"I can hear you, sir."

"What's the trouble?" It might be news of Chatworth. "Superintendent Cortland would like to see you, sir, some trouble at Haycourt Mews, that's all I know, sir."

"Right," said Roger, in a sharper voice. "I'm on my way."

"Just a minute, sir," the man said hastily, "here's another message for you ... It's from the Superintendent, will you please go straight to Haycourt Mews. One of our men's been badly hurt, that's all I know, sir."

## Chapter Eleven

# Missing

Roger didn't turn his car into Haycourt Mews, for as he passed the entrance, he saw half a dozen police cars already there. He pulled up about the spot where the killer car had been parked the other evening, and jumped out. Two uniformed men were on duty outside the flat. Plain-clothes men, all from the Yard, were marking off parts of the cobbled yard with paint. One was trying to take a plaster cast at a spot where dirt had piled up over the years. The photographers were packing up their cameras and tripods.

Big Bill Sloan appeared at the front door of the mews, hatless, red and rosy faced, obviously worried.

"Come up, Handsome, will you?"

"Coming, Bill." Roger went up the short flight of steps two at a time. His heart was beating uncomfortably fast, he felt a sense of anxiety and almost of guilt, for nothing should have been allowed to happen here. Why had it? He reached Sloan. "What's it all about?"

Sloan said simply, "Mrs. Jackson's missing. Our chap – young Hepple, you sent him – is at St. George's, and from the look of things he might not pull through."

"How was he hurt?"

"Battered about the head with a spanner," Sloan said. Between sentences he was very tight-lipped. "Nothing we can't handle, but Jackson's here, and we thought you—" He stopped.

Jackson appeared behind him, coming from the drawing-room. His eyes were glittering and his lips parted, showing his clenched teeth. There was sticking-plaster on his forehead and his nose, and his right eye was discoloured, but it was easy to forget all that as he drew level with Sloan.

"Any news of Rosemary?"

"Not yet," Roger said. "I—"

"West," Jackson grated, "I know how you people work, I know you'll work your guts out on this. *Find* her."

"We will." Somehow, Roger made that sound emphatic. "My God," Jackson said, clenching his hands tightly, "I can hardly believe it happened. I know your chap's in a bad way, but why the hell did he allow it to happen? Why? He was here to look after her, wasn't he? Why did he *allow* it?"

"We'll find out what happened and we'll find Mrs. Jackson," Roger said evenly, "and we may be much quicker than you think." Words, assurances – how much did they matter, how much did they help Jackson? "What time did this happen?"

Jackson began, "About twelve, I gather, I—"

"Let me give you both all the details," Sloan said, now big boy and uncle in one. He turned, and they went into the room where Roger had been last evening. Nothing had been touched, except that the ashtrays had been cleaned and the glasses taken away, the big cushions shaken. It was bright and as charming as ever. "Hepple was round here at nine o'clock. Mr. Jackson didn't leave until he'd arrived. He fixed the tape recorder to the telephone, and then went down into the mews, where he could watch the front door. We had a man in a house at the back, too, to watch the rear windows – we didn't leave anything to chance, Mr. Jackson."

Jackson nodded bleakly.

"According to a chauffeur who was washing down a car in a garage opposite, a man called here a little after twelve o'clock. The chauffeur saw him standing with his back to the mews, waiting for the door to open. He saw Hepple, our chap, move towards the steps – and the next thing the chauffeur knew, he was banged on the head, pushed inside and the garage doors were closed on him. They're the sliding type. The key was in the padlock on the outside, and he was locked in – when he came round, in five minutes or so, all he could do was shout and kick at the shutters. That's all he knows."

"Did Hepple say anything?" Roger asked quietly.

"He was unconscious when we found him," Sloan said. A milkman heard the chauffeur's rumpus, the chauffeur knew there was some funny business at the flat, and so they sent for us – 999. As Hepple wasn't about, our chaps broke in. They found Hepple just inside the hall, where he'd been dragged after he was attacked."

"And there isn't a sign of Rosemary," Jackson said fiercely, "not a sign."

She was alive.

And she could remember everything that had happened with nightmare clarity.

It had been such a promising morning for Rosemary Jackson, easily the happiest she had known for a long time. She felt quite sure that she and Charles were the victims of a plot, even though she couldn't imagine what it was about – unless it was revenge on the part of one of the men whom Charles had helped to send to prison. But the motive wasn't important to her. She was level-headed enough to persuade herself that now that the police were helping, the gravest danger was past.

She was anxious, that was all.

She'd watched Charles leave for the office, walking a little less briskly than usual; he had promised to take a taxi, and not walk. A detective had followed him. He shouldn't really have gone to the office, but some important cases were brewing; there always were. He'd waved from the corner where he had nearly been killed the previous night, and she had turned from the window and, for a while, watched the Scotland Yard detective fitting wires to the telephone cable so that everything said would be recorded on the tape machine.

"There's a little switch here, Ma'am," he said, touching one on the side of the recorder, "I should leave that switched on all the time. If you get a call and know it's nothing to do with this chap, switch off

– you won't waste the tape that way. Ever handled these records before?"

"Only in fun."

"Well, when you've finished this tape – that's if you do finish it, it will take three thousand words or so!" The detective grinned. He was pleasant if rather nondescript, with a slightly flabby chin, sparse dark hair and rather nice eyes. "Still, if the tape does run out, then you take it off like this."

He demonstrated slowly, and it was rather like changing a ribbon on a mammoth typewriter. "Then put the other on, like this." Again, he demonstrated. "Care to try, and make sure you've got it?"

Rosemary had three attempts before she was quite adept.

"That's all right now," Detective Officer Hepple said. "I'll wait outside I think, just in case anything happens. As Mr. West said this morning, though, it probably won't – the trouble with these jobs is that we never know about them and start watching until after the damage is done."

"I suppose so," Rosemary agreed.

She saw him out, and then busied herself about the flat. Now and again she looked out of the window to the lovely walled garden, where she noticed a gardener whom she hadn't seen before – a young man, instead of the old one who was usually there two or three days a week. She wondered if this was another C.I.D. man.

Just after twelve o'clock, when the kettle was on for a cup of tea, there was a ring at the front-door bell. It did not seriously occur to her that this might mean trouble, and in any case Hepple was in the mews, so she was in no danger.

She did not recognise the man who stood on the porch.

But she saw danger—

The man moved towards her swiftly. There was a small gun in his hand, hidden from the mews, visible only to her. A *gun*. Behind him, at the foot of the steps, was Hepple, obviously unaware of the gun. A moment later Hepple was hidden from her by the nearer man's head and shoulders.

Behind Hepple there was a second man, creeping.

Rosemary opened her mouth to scream. *"Mind!"* she cried. "There's—"

The man could kill her.

She saw the gun raised, saw the glitter in his eyes and felt absolutely certain that this was the man who had been in the car the night before. Then she heard a faint sneezing sound. A little whitish vapour billowed out of the muzzle of the gun, and enveloped her face. She felt gas stinging at her eyes and nose and mouth, and her scream was cut short. She backed desperately away and tried to slam the door, but was pushed roughly into the room. She couldn't see, the pain was so acute that she wanted to scream, but the gas made her catch her breath, and she could make only a sobbing sound. Then a man bundled her along the passage, into the kitchen, into the larder. She fell against the shelves with a clatter of tins, and the door was slammed, leaving her in darkness – but the darkness didn't matter, for tears streamed down her face, she could not see. She leaned against the wall, hands at her face, gasping for breath. The smarting gradually eased, but was still painful at her eyes and the back of her nose, and she felt as if she would choke.

She did not know how long she would stay there.

Suddenly, the door opened, and light came in, bright enough to hurt her eyes and make her close them tightly. She had seen the vague outline of the man's head and shoulders, that was all. She felt his hand, touching her wrist, and with sudden fury she struck out. She felt her fingers scratch across something soft – his face? – and then her wrist was twisted and she cried out in pain. The man growled something, she didn't know what, but next time she heard: "Come on, you bitch."

He was too strong for her, and dragged her towards the door. The front door was closed, but as he neared it, it opened an inch, and he called to someone outside: "Okay?"

"Yes," another man said. "Get a move on."

They were going to take her away.

There would be someone else in the mews, surely, someone who would help her. If she screamed it would be heard. She screwed herself up to the point of screaming, was ready to as soon as the front door opened, and then she kicked against something and tripped and nearly fell.

It was the detective, Hepple, with his head and face bloodied as he lay inert.

"Try anything, and that's what will happen to you," the man said in her ear, and dragged her forward. She stepped over the body, realising that Hepple might be dead.

As it was, he seemed to have taken away all hope.

The door opened wide, and daylight hurt her eyes.

Then the man thrust a handkerchief, rolled into a ball, inside her mouth. She couldn't scream or cry out, but choked as he hustled her down the stairs and towards a small, black car – an Austin Iso – which stood outside. She felt sure it was the car which had nearly run Charles down. The rear door stood wide open, with a man at the door – a smallish man with a pale face. She was helped inside, pushed into a corner and then joined by the man.

The doors slammed.

The other man took the wheel.

Rosemary kept trying to speak, trying to get the handkerchief out of her mouth, but it was wet and soggy and she could not move it. Then she felt a painful stab on her fore-arm; on the instant she suspected a hypodermic injection. She tried to struggle, but the man held her down. Gradually she stopped trying, and sat in the corner. She saw the passers-by, knew that if she could scream or even beckon to them they would help; but there was nothing she could do.

Soon, there was nothing that she wanted to do, for she felt a strange lassitude.

It took the pain away from her eyes and mouth and nose – and from her wrist, which the man had twisted so badly. It stole over her limbs. It was more than lassitude, it was a kind of peacefulness. She forgot what had happened to her, and she forgot fear. Something quite wonderful was happening to her. It was as if she was being carried away from the ordinary world into a world of new delights. She had never known anything like this. It suspended thought, and brought only a sensation of great well-being, almost of elation. She was aware of the smooth running of the car, yet she did not really notice it; nor did she notice where they were going, the streets they were passing.

She closed her eyes; to dream.

Everything was dreamlike and wonderful, even while she was being helped from the car and into a large house which stood in a large garden. A man was at her side all the time – the man who had once frightened her but now seemed part of this new, wonderful world.

She was taken to a bedroom.

She lay down, felt someone loosening her belt, and taking off her shoes. It was snug and warm and lovely. She knew that she was alone, and she wanted to be alone, with these dreams which were not so much dreams as sensations.

She went to sleep.

When she woke, her mouth was sore, so was her nose, and her eyes were tingling. She had a completely different feeling, of acute depression, the kind of feeling she would sometimes have when things went wrong between her and Charles, or after she had received one of those typewritten or telephoned messages.

She longed for the dream state.

Gradually, she became even more irritable, and became frightened again; her reactions now were quite normal. She had been drugged, of course – with heroin or something like it. She was sure, because when Charles had been drawing up the committee's report on dangerous drugs, she had studied the subject, and—

Was *that* anything to do with this? Was Charles's part in that report the reason for his danger?

The thought, as well as what had happened to her, was terrifying.

So was her helplessness.

She got off the bed, almost in panic, the wonderful dreams turned into nightmares. She went to the window, and found the glass was frosted so that she could not see out. She looked desperately for a catch with which to open it, but there was none; it was a dummy window.

## Chapter Twelve

# The Parson in Person

"The truth is that we aren't any nearer finding your wife than we were this morning, and I've got to admit it," Roger West said to Jackson. "I'm desperately sorry." He paused, to give the solicitor a chance to speak, but Jackson only stared at him, with burning eyes. They were in Roger's office at Scotland Yard at six o'clock that evening. "We know that she went off in a black Austin Iso, but we haven't the number of the car or anything else to help us identify it. We know that it turned into Grosvenor Square, but that's the last we've been able to find out. The Iso is one of the most popular cars in the country, and black's the most popular colour."

He paused again.

Jackson said, "What about the driver?"

"All we know, and it isn't much help, is that he was a smallish man dressed in dark grey. The Rolls-Royce chauffeur saw only his back, a man about five feet six tall, narrow shouldered, wearing a dark-grey trilby hat and black shoes. That would fit thousands of men, hundreds of them driving Iso cars."

"What are you doing about it?" Jackson growled.

"Every man in London is alerted, and all the Home Counties are co-operating. Any black Iso which is seen in unusual circumstances will be reported, but it would be hypocritical to tell you that we've much hope, from the information now available."

"What else are you doing?"

"By tomorrow morning, every newspaper in the country will carry your wife's photograph, a description of the car and of the man," Roger said. "Every way we know of tracing a missing person is being used."

"Including hospitals and morgues?" Jackson's voice was harsh.

"Including hospitals and morgues," admitted Roger, and for the first time felt that he could ease this man's almost intolerable burden. He did so with deliberate casualness, taking out cigarettes as he spoke and offering them. "Not that I've any real fear of finding her dead. If they'd wanted to kill her, they could have done it at the flat. Obviously they wanted to kidnap her."

He lit the flame of hope.

"I suppose you're right," Jackson said slowly, and took a cigarette. "Thanks." They lit up. "But why the hell should they want to kidnap her? There isn't a reason in the world."

"Oh, there's a reason," Roger said briskly. "When we find it we'll be nearer the men who took her off. We're still after people with their knife into you too. We've checked the two whose names you gave us, the pair who shouted vengeance after they'd been sentenced. One is dead, the other came out of jail to find his wife had taken a little poultry farm in the country, and as far as we can trace he's completely reformed – his wife sees to that. In any case, he doesn't answer any of the descriptions we have."

Jackson said, "It couldn't look much blacker. West—"

He paused for a moment, then went on abruptly, "What can I do? I can't possibly work – my partners understand that I've got to try to do something to find Rosemary."

That had been inevitable.

"The thing you can do is go back over everything in your life and try to find out if you've ever given cause for anyone to hate you like this. And if you're satisfied that there's no one, then probe into your wife's past. Do you really know much about it?"

Jackson hesitated.

"Not much," he admitted at last. "We met almost by chance – she was at a cocktail party at a friend's house. She didn't have much of an early life, her father died when she was young, and her mother struggled to put her through college. I know her schools, that kind of thing, but—"

"Is her mother still alive?"

"Yes, she lives in Oxford – God knows what she'll feel when she learns about this," Jackson added abruptly. "I telephoned a friend of hers soon after I heard, and I ought to go and tell her myself. But I can't believe there's anything in Rosemary's past to warrant—" He broke off.

"I'll do what I can," he said at last, "but if there's any other thing you think I can do, for God's sake tell me."

"We will," promised Roger briskly. "Sit down with pencil and paper and recall everything you can remember of your association with Councillor Mrs. Kitt while you were at Ligate, particularly what you can remember of this particular case." He took a press cutting from his wallet, a copy of one of those found in the mess at Mrs. Kitt's room. "I've got Connolly working on this, too, but you might find some angle that he's missed."

Jackson read the report.

"Offhand, I don't remember it." He was quiet for a few seconds, and then went on slowly, "I don't know, though—I do remember. There'd been half a dozen nasty accidents near that spot in Ligate, and a kind of unofficial Watch Committee was kicking up a hell of a fuss. It was near the power-station, you know the place, and there were two nasty corners. This was early morning – nine-ish – and few people were about. It was the unofficial committee which really insisted on a case. I thought the police allowed their hands to be forced too much – unless Connolly thought that if he brought the case and the defendant was acquitted, it might draw the Watch Committee's teeth." Jackson was silent for a moment, and obviously his mind was working very quickly; eagerly. "Yes, I remember. The victim was a young woman, pregnant if I remember rightly – yes, that's right, she was – that's why the case had a lot of public attention. You know how dreamy women can get, and how sluggish when they're carrying. Apparently she got off the bus and then stepped past the back of it, right into the path of a Jaguar coming in the other direction. She was badly knocked about, and the child was stillborn. I took the driver's defence," Jackson went on abruptly. "There was some argument in the office about whether we should, as there was so much sentiment on the injured woman's side – the charge was of causing injury by careless driving. The unofficial Watch Committee put up several witnesses for the prosecution, but I had a pick of the witnesses for the defence. There was a middle-aged woman, I forget her name, quiet, self-possessed type who was just behind the bus. The absolutely reliable kind of witness. Then there was the police officer who actually saw the thing happen – he was just going off duty. I remember him well, one of the stolid, portentous type, but with a wonderful eye – chap invaluable on traffic control. Head like pieces of wood, except—"

Roger said very softly, "Do you remember his name?"

"Yes, it's all coming back. Atkinson. He was moved a few weeks before I left Ligate, went out Clapham way. Totting, somewhere like that. He—" Jackson broke off abruptly.

Roger was getting up from his chair. There were moments when it was impossible to hide excitement, and this was one. Here was the common factor which affected all of the people concerned – Atkinson, too. That name, that type of copper and the fact that he'd gone to the south-west of London made it practically certain that the witness had been Sergeant Atkinson. He could almost picture the scene. The young woman, the Jaguar, the screeching of brakes and the screaming of women, the stolid police officer, the equally stolid and dependable Mrs. Bray – and later, Jackson acting for the defence in his brisk and effective way, and Mrs. Kitt saying what she thought of the prosecution's case in no uncertain way.

"This Watch Committee," Roger said, "do you remember the people in it?"

"I can't say I do," said Jackson, after a pause. "I remember vaguely what their witnesses were like, but can only give you one name. You can get the others from the records, of course."

"Who's the one?"

"The parson who still beats the air about road accidents – the newspapers call him Parson Pete," Jackson said. "Same chap that

Rosemary was talking about last night, he was actually here with her a few weeks ago, and—"

He broke off, catching his breath.

"He couldn't be—"

"I think I'll go and see Parson Pete now," Roger said very softly. "Will you get busy on that statement?"

"West, I really ought to go and see Rosemary's mother." Jackson was fighting against the desire to talk of the parson. "I shan't stay, of course, but if I leave now I'll be at her place by half-past eight, and can get back about midnight. Will the morning do for the stuff you want?"

"Yes," said Roger, "but if you remember anything that seems significant, telephone the Yard or me. I gave you my home telephone number this afternoon, didn't I?"

"I've got it somewhere," Jackson said, and looked through his wallet. "Ah, here it is. West—" He gulped, suddenly, and then turned away; obviously tears were very close to the surface of his eyes. "Oh, what's the use of needling you, I know you'll do your damnedest."

He left soon afterwards, in a Riley, with a police car following; police along the main road to Oxford were alerted, too.

When he had gone, Roger telephoned the Ligate Divisional Headquarters. Connolly had left, but a brisk Inspector promised to get out all the statements on the Watch Committee's case against the Jaguar driver. It couldn't easily be done tonight, as it meant getting help from the clerk of the court.

"Get it, will you?" asked Roger. "It could be vital. Ever hear anything of that Watch Committee these days?"

"Oh, it broke up soon after the case," said the Inspector. "Only good it did was to get a traffic island put up near that spot, which was something. I'd just come into the Division, so I know about it more from hearsay than from recollection. I'll get those names and addresses, though. Parson Pete was its leader – chairman and secretary and what-have-you."

"Thanks," said Roger. "I'll see him."

He had read a lot about Parson Pete – or the Reverend Peter Waite – during the day.

The man was still young, in his middle thirties, a Nonconformist minister of a remote little sect – his "Reverend" was a courtesy title rather than the mark of any religious training. His name of Waite was one of those odd little ironies, for his life's record was one of burning impatience. All reports about him were much the same. He was a pleasant-looking, well-spoken, good-tempered and generous man, prominent on many social-service committees, and a leader of a Boy Scout troop. No one had ever breathed a word against his reputation – in fact, he would have been extremely popular but for his one fanatical weakness: his bitter attitude towards road accidents.

Road accidents, he asserted, were murder; and all murderers should be treated alike.

The church to which he belonged had only a few branches, one at Ligate, another at Totting, and he had been minister at Totting for three years. He lived in one of the large houses overlooking the Fields, and like many of its neighbours, the house was divided into flats. He used part of his flat as Campaign Rooms for the anti-accident campaign, and from there he issued leaflets and posters and presumably wrote his letters – like the one which he had first sent to Rosemary Jackson, before calling on her.

Coincidence?

Roger reached the house a little after seven o'clock that night. He was in a mood that was nearly savage. Just before leaving the Yard there'd been a message from the hospital about Chatworth, and it offered very little hope. Roger had always realised Chatworth's importance in the affairs of the Criminal Investigation Department, but had never realised quite how great it was. There wasn't an officer or man of any length of service who didn't show something of his depression.

Roger felt it almost too heavily.

He had told the Totting police that he would be going, and met P.C. Davis at a corner, by appointment – the corner near the spot where Atkinson had been killed. Davis was with a sergeant, but a man who was quite willing to keep in the background and let Davis say his piece.

"I've made two attempts, sir, but haven't been able to find any special association between Sergeant Atkinson and Parson P – I mean Mr. Waite, sir. Mrs. Atkinson remembers him from the Ligate days, and the sergeant often had a moan about him, but that's about all."

"I see. How is Mrs. Atkinson?"

"She's got a sister with her, down from Manchester," said Davis. "I think things will be a bit better along there now. But I shall keep in touch."

"And keep me in touch, too," Roger said. "Do you know if Waite's in?"

"He was seen to come in early this afternoon, sir," put in the Sergeant, "and he hasn't been observed leaving the house."

"Only one way out?"

"That's all, sir – two gates, both leading into this road."

"Good, thanks. I don't expect any trouble, I just want a talk with him, but leave a man handy so that I can call on him if needs be. Is Davis on his beat, or free?"

"At your service, sir," the sergeant said.

"Good, thanks. Let's go up to the flat, Davis," Roger said, and they entered the dark grounds, with some small trees and thick bushes growing round the walls and in a circular patch in the middle of the carriage-way, which showed up pale against the surrounding darkness. A light was on inside the house, showing against the front-door fanlight, but none was at any of the windows. Davis shone his torch as they reached the porch, and it showed on several bell-pushes and on cards pinned above them.

*Flat 6: Mr. Peter Waite*
*Anti-Road Murder Campaign H.Q.*

"He really goes all out for it, sir, doesn't he?"

"Yes." Roger pressed a bell, and a moment later there was a harsh buzzing and a click, as the front door opened.

"Lot of protection that is, if he lets you in without finding out who's calling," went on Davis. "He might be expecting someone, though. Want me here or upstairs, sir?"

"On the top landing, I think."

"Right, sir."

There were dim lights at the two landings, the paintwork of the doors and the banisters was in such a bad condition that it had flaked off in many places, and the walls – painted too – were showing big patches where the paint was flaking off. Boards creaked beneath cracked linoleum. There were two downstairs flats, two on the next floor, two on the top. There was no sound from any of them, and it was gloomy enough to seem uncanny.

"Here we are, sir," said Davis, and shone his torch on the numeral 6 on a dark door. "I'll keep out of sight when he comes."

"Good," said Roger.

Yes, Davis would make a good C.I.D. man.

Roger pressed the bell in the middle of the door, and it rang very loudly. After a pause, footsteps came, then a click as if a light had been switched on. Next moment the door opened wide, and a youthful-looking man with a fuzz of fair hair stood there, eyes rounded, lips parted as if in surprise.

"Good evening," Roger said formally. "Are you Mr. Waite?"

"I—well—yes, I am," said Parson Pete, "I'm Waite, yes." He seemed almost bewildered, disappointed. "Can I—er—how can I help you? If you've come for the meeting, I'm afraid that is tomorrow night, but if you would like some posters and leaflets—" He stopped, giving the impression that he did not really think that the caller had come for the Campaign leaflets.

"I'd like a word with you," said Roger, and took out his card. He held it out, studying the other man as he glanced down.

The Reverend Peter Waite was thinner than his newspaper photographs had suggested. He still looked boyish, and had full, rather red lips. He frowned as he looked at the card, and gave the impression that he was short-sighted. He wore a loose-fitting clerical collar and a light-grey suit, which puckered at the shoulders, as if it had been wet through at some time or other, and rough-dried.

He looked up. "From Scotland *Yard*? Chief Inspector West? Surely I've heard – but come in, Chief Inspector, come in. I was expecting someone else, a young lady as a matter of fact, and I admit that I'm a little disappointed, but perhaps I'm expecting her too early –she said about half-past seven, and it isn't quite half-past yet, is it? I hope this matter won't take too long, Miss Akers and I were going—er—out."

"I don't think it need take long," said Roger.

Miss Akers?

He stepped inside.

There was a little cubicle of a passage with three doors leading off it. One door was wide open, and beyond it was a light much brighter than any other Roger had seen here. It shone on a wall which was covered with posters and slogans – mostly in bright colours, many of them very crude, as if children had drawn them. Also in sight was a row of shelves built against the wall, and on these were stacks of leaflets.

"We—er—can go into my living-room," Waite said almost nervously. "More comfortable chairs, and—"

"I'm interested in your campaign headquarters," Roger said, and stepped into the brightly lit room. It was much larger than he had expected, and every wall was papered with crude Campaign drawings. Red and green were the prominent colours. In the middle of the room were four trestle tables, placed together to make one large table, and on these were piles of envelopes, pens and ink – and there were four chairs. A small desk with a chair backing on the big bay window was at one end of the room. On this were papers and a small, grey portable typewriter.

"Rather like election campaign rooms," Roger said more easily.

"Oh, do you think so?" Waite had a rather precise way of talking. "So long as it gives the impression of activity, Chief Inspector, that is the important thing. When helpers come I feel sure they're encouraged by the evidence that there have been others before them – as if the chair has been held vacant just for them while they are able to work. Do you—er— know much about my campaign, Chief Inspector? I—but I mustn't get on to my pet hobby horse, you've business with me! How *can* I help you?"

Roger was still looking round.

"How many of the people who helped in your early days are still with you, Mr. Waite?"

"Eh? Oh, early helpers. Well, two or three have been loyal throughout, but I started in Ligate as possibly you know, and it is too far away for people to travel. One or two happened to move nearer, and they come regularly, but I confess that public support is very small. Lamentably small, in fact."

Roger studied him; and gave him time to get worked up.

Something was happening to him; a kind of transformation. It was a strange thing to see. The expression in the big, rather childlike eyes became compelling, as if he was willing Roger to listen. He gripped the lapels of his coat tightly, as he might when addressing a meeting, not an individual. Thus he made a slightly pathetic figure, yet there was a dignity about him. His voice grew harder and seemed more deep, too.

"One of the awful ironies in the human being is his fear for himself and his cold-heartedness towards others. Oh, there is some compassion, I grant you, but – what use is compassion to men, to women, to little children, crushed under the wheels of a car, mangled, disfigured or disabled for life – or killed? *Killed*. Compassion does not serve them, sir, compassion is an empty cup whenever it is offered them. What is wanted is not compassion for the victims but a declaration of war upon the slayers of men, a countrywide cry of horror against the slaughter on our roads, millions of people roused to force the hand of the Government, to compel them to legislate as they should have done years ago – to compel them to regard a killer at the wheel as they regard a murderer. For what else *is* he?"

Now, those eyes were glowing with the light of a great passion, and with one hand raised, the finger pointing to the sky, this little man cried: "Tell me that! What else is he but a murderer who may kill with impunity, and maim and lame? Why should he not suffer as other murderers suffer? Tell me—*why?*"

## Chapter Thirteen

## The Parson Speaks

Waite's voice rang round the room. He looked exalted, as if he believed that his words were inspired, and the inspiration was working within him now. One finger still pointed heavenwards, his eyes glittered and shone, his mouth was open as if he wanted to repeat the word time and time again.

"*Why?*" he cried.

"I think I could tell you why," Roger said very quietly, "but there are times—"

"Oh, I have never met a policeman who did not defend the laxity with which they enforce even the laws we do have against criminal driving," said Waite abruptly. The metamorphosis was very quick this time, but he wasn't quite so placid as he had been before the outburst. "I suppose that is understandable, it cannot be easy. But if I could get the support of some influential body—" He broke off abruptly, only to demand, "Tell me this, do your men *like* what they have to do after these fearful accidents? Do they *like* bending over crushed flesh and bones, do they like—?"

"No, they don't." The sharpness of Roger's voice stopped Waite on the instant. "We don't look upon motorists as a race of murderers, either. If you would moderate your campaign you might get more support."

"That's exactly what they *all* say," Waite said. "Water it down, water it down, make the law full of loopholes so that killers can escape scot free. The law is as much to blame as the motorist, the cyclist, the lunatic pedestrian who steps into the road. Chief Inspector, have you ever studied my proposals? Have you ever spared so much as a minute of your valuable time to find out what I am suggesting, and what I campaign for? *Have* you?"

"Not specifically."

"At least you have the honesty to admit it," said Waite, in that husky soft voice. "Most people pretend that they know exactly what I mean, when in fact they have read the headlines of the newspapers and dismissed me as a blaspheming and hypocritical fanatic. Well they might, if they judge only from what they read in the newspapers, and they do that, Chief Inspector. Look. *Look at these!*" He spun round vigorously, and the fire was in his eyes again. He strode to the shelves and snatched up a leaflet from each pile, five in all, then he swung round and thrust them into Roger's hand. "Take them, read them, find out what I am trying to do before you tell your policemen to dismiss me as a ranting lunatic. I tell you, Chief Inspector, that the crime of a motorist who is careless on the road and, as a consequence of his carelessness, kills a human being, is as like murder as brother may be like brother, and the motorist should be punished as severely. Yes, as *severely*. Thou shalt not kill, saith the Lord – and motorists are killing people at this very moment – outside this very gate only a few hours ago an officer was run down in the execution of his duty. What do you think of that, Chief Inspector? Because a motor vehicle was used as the lethal weapon, do you regard it as less wicked than it would have been had the man been killed with a gun or a hammer?"

He drew very close, now, his wide-set eyes blazing. There was a little bubbly froth at the corners of his lips, and he spluttered as he talked. His vehemence could not fail to impress – and it could not fail to cause disquiet. Here was a man talking from the very depth of his heart, out of a passionate conviction and a burning, almost evangelical zeal.

"Well," he demanded, "how do you reckon that policeman's death, Chief Inspector? Read my leaflets, read my proposals, satisfy yourself that I am not simply an idiot, bleating. The proposals are simplicity itself. If a man be tried and found guilty of killing another through carelessness or negligence of any kind, then – God forgive me I have not yet the courage to propose greater punishment – let him spend the next five years in prison. If he causes injury, one year. If he causes lesser injuries, then he shall receive lesser penalties – but none less than six months' imprisonment, Chief Inspector. Look at me!" Roger was already eyeing him steadily, trying to assess him dispassionately and yet feeling strangely moved. *"Look at me,* Chief Inspector, and tell me that you think that if such punishments were the law's retribution for careless driving, you believe that men would continue to drive carelessly?"

He paused; and then he shook Roger's arm and almost spat the question out again.

"Do you think they would? Answer me!"

"No," Roger said very slowly, "I don't think they would." Waite dropped his hands.

"Thank you," he said, "thank you for that measure of honesty. It is refreshing. Most people are so shocked that they raise foolish arguments, such as saying that in practice it would not work out, that it would be unfair on a man who makes one mistake – unfair! In God's name what do they think it is to the man who died, to the wives and children who suffer, what—" Waite broke off; almost choking.

Then he turned away and, trembling, went to the four trestle tables, where the white envelopes lay and the pens and ink were idle, and he leaned on a corner of the table and wiped his forehead. He was sweating freely, and his voice was unsteady as he went on: "I must ask you to forgive me, Chief Inspector; it is not often these days that I lose my self-control like this. Sometimes, of course, sometimes – and especially when I was younger, just after she was killed, I was almost insane. I wanted to take people by the scruff of their necks and bang their silly heads together until they realised that they were condoning murder." He paused again, gulped, and took out a spotless handkerchief and wiped his forehead. "But by painful experience, I found that you cannot shock people into taking action. I tried to win converts by persuasion. I called meeting after meeting, I approached members of the clergy, doctors, local officials, local councillors, Members of Parliament, members of the House of Lords, yes, I even importuned the Crown. Sometimes, I had a little encouragement. Once or twice committees were formed to consider my proposals, but sooner or later each one collapsed. At one time I had a Watch Committee of alert and vigilant people, but their efforts failed. The police defended men who drove cars as if they were blowing up toy balloons. Magistrates everywhere found drivers, cyclists, even pedestrians guilty of causing death or injury to others by their carelessness and – sometimes – *sometimes,* mark you, they fined the killer a few guineas. A few pounds!"

He stopped again.

All his intensity was back; so was the glitter in his eyes.

"Go on, Chief Inspector," he said thinly, "tell me what every policeman I have discussed this with tells me. Tell me what everyone seems to think is the soothing drug of folly. Tell me that a man's *conscience* punishes him. And let me tell you that until this slaughter on the roads is stopped, it will make a mockery of all that men say they believe, all man's vaunted humanity. It is a slap in the face of God, a curse upon our children. And it can be stopped! Give me dictatorial powers and I will stop it overnight. I will frighten men and women into taking care. There is no other way."

He was quivering, as if he was cold; but it was warm in here.

Roger waited, watching him carefully.

"You haven't said much, Chief Inspector," Waite said at last. "You have been more patient and more courteous than most; they find some pretext to interrupt me. Now – what *can* I do for you?"

"How are you campaigning now, Mr. Waite?" Roger asked mildly.

"You may well ask," the parson said. He looked ruefully about the big, nearly empty room. "I am writing personal letters to the relatives of the victims of road accidents, and trying to engage their support, as well as writing to Members of Parliament and to the local newspapers, but – few of them trouble to answer. I have not the heart to write to people at the time of their bereavement, and they seem to forget so soon. So very soon. A few come here and work. Last night I had a meeting here. My committee is nominally thirty strong, and seven attended." He raised his hands, in a helpless little gesture, and went on, "You see? And yet I am right, I am positive that I am right. This mass slaughter could be stopped almost overnight."

He glanced past Roger towards the door, as if he had heard a sound there, and for a moment he looked eager – and obviously ready to hurry to open the door. But there was no sound after all, and he looked back at Roger.

"I keep asking you, how can I help you?" His voice had become subdued, dispirited.

Roger said quietly, "I'm not sure. I'm trying to get details of an accident that happened in Ligate nearly four years ago. You and some of your Watch Committee were witnesses for the prosecution."

"We often were, Chief Inspector."

"This was a woman named Rawley, a young woman who was pregnant, and—"

"Oh, Mrs. *Raw*ley," said Waite, and closed his eyes. "Mrs. Rawley," he repeated, and moved away towards the small desk. He sat on this, which was more solid and comfortable, and pushed the little typewriter away with his right hand. Roger glanced at the machine. It was a "Cono", probably twenty years old.

Now that he was nearer, Roger was able to see that it was the same type and period as the machine on which the letters to Rosemary Jackson had been typed.

By it were some envelopes, the addresses already typed in.

"Mrs. Rawley," repeated Waite for the second time, and he sounded near despair. "It is strange you should select that particular case, Chief Inspector. It was the one on which I had more public support than at any time, either before or since. The circumstances were so sad, the mother with her child soon to be born, a pretty girl, too, and very well known in Ligate. I had excellent witnesses. I worked on that case as I have never worked before. In fact, I think it was the case that nearly broke my spirit."

"What was so unusual about it?" Roger asked.

"At first, nothing," said Waite. "The witnesses for the defence were very strong. The Bench showed its customary hostility to my unofficial Watch Committee. The verdict was 'Not Guilty'. There was a public outcry for a few days, but soon it was all forgotten, and then—then." went on the little parson, "I realised that it was the one case I should not have tried to win, because it was *her* fault. Mrs. Rawley was to blame. It wasn't the driver's fault at all. I interviewed many people before I came to the conclusion that the very test case on which I had built such hopes was an unjust one. Could irony be more bitter, Chief Inspector?"

"No," Roger said slowly, "that must have been as cruel as it can get. About this Watch Committee – did it disband?"

"Yes. And soon afterwards I left Ligate – because of the case, I knew that I had no further hope of getting results there, but I had to go on with my efforts. I couldn't give up a campaign – a *crusade* – simply because of one mistake. But it was from that time onwards that I began to lose influential support. There had been some, and one newspaper actually advanced some money. I had thousands of members of my League, too, all paying a little towards the expenses. I could have posters printed and put up, produce leaflets by the hundred thousand. I had a small paid staff, too. Now I rely on irregular voluntary help, and the only posters I can afford are those which children paint in Sunday School competitions."

He stopped, in the midst of his own bitterness.

But he hadn't let himself be beaten. A thousand people would have given up, but not this thin, frail-looking man with the sad eyes.

"Mr. Waite," Roger said quietly, and paused.

"Yes?"

"When I first joined the Police Force, a woman was murdered in Epping Forest," Roger said. "Eighteen years afterwards, I helped to trace the murderer, who is now in prison on a life sentence. I thought that recollection might interest you."

Waite stood very still, his hands raised a little higher than his waist, his legs parted, like a boxer almost ready to go into the attack. His eyes grew very bright; glowing. It was a long time before he said: "I don't know what brought you here, Chief Inspector, but thank God you came. I confess that I was on the point of giving up completely. I have been working on this campaign for nearly ten years, and felt that I couldn't go on much longer. You shame me. I accept the reproof. Eighteen years or eighty years, what does it matter? Whether I see it accomplished in my lifetime or not, what does it matter? Do you know what began it, Chief Inspector?"

"I would like to."

"This," said Waite, and moved towards a photograph which stood on the mantelpiece. It was very faded. The sepia brown was yellowing in patches, like the newspaper cutting which had been framed with it. It said briefly:

"Mrs. L. L. Waite, of 85, Ardith Road, was run over by a private car on Friday afternoon, and received injuries which have since proved fatal. An inquest will be held."

"Who?" asked Roger.

"My mother."

Well, it added up; it even made a kind of sense. The woman in the picture looked young and rather charming, a little old-world, as one might expect of this man's mother.

"I see," Roger said. "Now—"

There was a sound outside, this time unmistakable. Waite moved quickly away; the living had suddenly become more important than the dead. Then came a ring at the front-door bell, and Roger studied the man's eagerness as he hurried to open it – but he didn't just stand idle. He moved to the desk and picked up three of the envelopes, thrust two into his pocket, and studied the third. He wanted a crooked lower-case "c", a slightly broken capital "E" and a "v" which dropped lower than most of the letters on the line.

He heard Waite say: "So you have come, you really meant it," and heard a girl say: "Of course." He was out of sight of the door then, and had time to see that the lower-case "c" and the capital "E" were identical with those on the letters which Rosemary Jackson had received.

Those letters had been typed here; or else on this machine.

In every part of England the hunt was on for Rosemary Jackson. Her photograph had been sent to all London and Home Counties police stations, evening newspapers throughout the country had carried it, with an urgent request for anyone who had seen her to report to the nearest police station.

Already reports were reaching stations as far apart as Plymouth and Liverpool. While Roger West was at Waite's apartment, dozens of policemen were interviewing dozens of "witnesses" – but Rosemary Jackson was not found.

She was in London.

She was dreaming beautiful dreams.

## Chapter Fourteen

## June Akers

Roger slipped the third envelope into his pocket, with the others, and looked up at the door. He couldn't be sure whether they were coming straight in or not. He pictured Waite's face when he had been so carried away, remembered the froth at his lips, all the signs that the man was a fanatic. Fanaticism could border on madness, and—

Madmen could be cunning, too.

This man could be mad.

If Waite were asked straight out who had access to that typewriter, he might lie. Asked who came here to help with the Campaign, he might tell the truth. It would be far better to try to find out who came here without letting Waite know what was being done.

These envelopes would justify a search warrant.

Waite came in with his hand on the arm of a young woman. She had a round face, pleasant features and very clear grey eyes, and was dressed in a well-tailored suit; nothing gave the impression that she lived in a poorly-furnished apartment in a carved-up house near the Fields; the touch of quality in everything about her was unmistakable. But that wasn't the reason for Roger's sharp interest.

This was the girl whose photograph was in Mrs. Kitt's room; this was Mrs. Kitt's niece.

"June, allow me to present Chief Inspector West of Scotland Yard," Waite said, with a return to his earlier preciseness. "Chief Inspector, I would like you to meet Miss June Akers."

"How are you?" Roger said, and gave no hint of his surprise.

"How're you?" June Akers didn't look startled at the sight of a Yard officer, but Waite might have prepared her for the meeting. She looked – nice. A parson's-wife type? That was going too far, and yet her smile had a kind of quietness which might well serve such a man as Waite, and she glanced at him with obvious affection.

Too obvious? Remember she was Mrs. Kitt's niece.

"The Chief Inspector is interested in my original Watch Committee, June," Waite said, "but I don't think he'll keep us long. Will you, Chief Inspector?"

"If you can give me the names and addresses of that committee, and the address of Mr. Rawley, I needn't keep you a minute longer."

"Gladly, gladly," said Waite, now cheerfulness itself. "And it won't take very long. I don't want to appear inhospitable, but Miss Akers and I were planning to go to a film together, at the Granada. We're a little late, but the main picture is the one we're anxious to see. We don't often – but I'll get those names and addresses. At least I can say I'm methodical," he added, as he went to the filing-cabinet and opened one of the small drawers at the top. "I've a complete list of all the men and women who have ever offered help or contributed funds – several thousands of them. The genuine workers and committee members are in a separate section at the front, it's quite easy to copy them out. I can put my finger on those you want in a jiffy. I've no doubt you have your notebook!" He gave a quick, almost bashful smile, and was obviously very self-conscious with the girl present. "Now—perhaps you'd like to copy them down."

Roger began, using abbreviated longhand.

This was really a waste of time, for as soon as the pair was out of here he would be on the telephone to Divisional H.Q., asking for a search warrant. He would get one in a matter of half an hour or so, any local Justice of the Peace would sign it. Then with Davis and a couple of other men he would go over these records thoroughly, but leave no sign of their searching. After that, the house must be watched day and night until the end of the case.

He felt the old, familiar throbbing of excitement at the thought of being on the verge of results.

He finished his notes.

"Now I'll leave you to go to the pictures," he said brightly, and added as if in an afterthought: "Perhaps I can give you a lift."

"It's very kind of you," Waite began.

The girl smiled. "I've a car downstairs."

Waite ushered Roger to the door. The girl seemed to be in no great hurry, and certainly wasn't perturbed. There was no sign of Davis as the door opened or even when it closed, but as soon as it did, the constable whispered from the stairs: "Everything all right, sir?"

"Yes, Davis, fine. Did you come on your motor cycle?"

"Yes, sir, it's parked round the corner."

"Go and get it," said Roger, "and follow Waite and the girl who's just gone in to see him. A Miss June Akers. They say they're going to the Granada Theatre – I'd like to make sure." "Right, sir," said Davis. "Anything else?"

"Come back here—no, you'll be near H.Q. if they do go to the pictures, so go there. Still ready for a turn of duty?"

"Night and day if needs be."

"Good. Look slippy, then. Don't take any notice of me as I come out."

Davis hurried down the bottom flight of stairs, and Roger felt the keen air sweep in as the front door was opened and the man went out. He didn't close the door. Roger stepped on to the porch. It was much colder than it had been, and the stars were hidden by heavy clouds, but there was sufficient light from the fanlight and from nearby lamps to show the couple getting into a pale-coloured car.

Davis followed them.

Ten minutes later, Roger turned into the main entrance of Divisional Headquarters, and was saluted by the sergeant on duty as he hurried up the stairs to the Night Inspector's office. He didn't know who it would be, but that didn't matter – all he wanted was someone to get a move on. He tapped at the door and went in on the "come in" – to find a small, fuggy office, a positive haze of pipe smoke and a big man in his shirt-sleeves sitting at a desk which seemed all telephones and scattered documents.

Through this haze there showed a man with a large, long, red face, a pair of heavy-lidded eyes, a double chin and a fat neck eased because his tie was undone. The ends of a bright-blue tie hung down, and the buttonholes of his neckband and shirt looked as if someone had been at them with scissors.

This was Chief Inspector Carter, until recently at the Yard.

"Cor," he greeted. "Honoured, I'm sure." He made a mock salute and rose an inch from his chair. "Take a pew. I heard you were around and about, but I didn't think you'd, condescend to come and have a word with me. What can't you do by yourself?"

"Hallo, Alf," said Roger, and sat on a small, empty desk where a sergeant worked by day. "When you've finished filling in your football pools, tell me if you've a tame magistrate near, will you?"

"Want a search warrant?"

"Yes."

"Grounds?"

"A typewriter in a certain local house is the typewriter on which certain poison-pen letters have been written, and there is reason to believe—"

Carter's heavy lids rose so much that they seemed to disappear into the man's forehead.

"Waite's?"

"Yes."

"I thought he—well, anyway, there's a tame magistrate about five minutes' drive away from here, I'll come with you. Just a search warrant?"

"Yes. Who've you got here who can make a good job of breaking and entering?" asked Roger, as Carter pushed his chair back against the wall, stood up and began to pull the ends of his collar and shirt together. "I'd like to get into Waite's place, photograph the records that he's got at the flat and then get away without him or anyone else knowing what we've been doing."

"Hmm," said Carter, and squinted down his nose in a futile effort to see whether his tie was straight. "Well, I dunno. Wilson—no, he's off with flu. Charlesworth might mess it up – Handsome, I hate to say it, but I think you ought to send for someone from the Yard; my night chaps are a bit heavy-handed, and it'll take as long to get day chaps out as it will to get your experts over. Get them on the move a bit, too, instead of sitting on their—"

"May I telephone?" Roger asked dryly, and moved forward; before Carter had shrugged himself into a big brown tweed coat, Roger was speaking to the Yard. He arranged for two men to meet him near Waite's house in an hour's time. The show at the Granada would not be over for at least another two hours, there should be plenty of time.

"I'm ready," said Carter. "What we do for you chaps at the Yard! Really think you've got something on the parson?"

"I think we might get something from his campaign records," Roger said. "Anything in for me?"

"No," said Carter, "we had a couple of phoney reports about Rosemary Jackson. Wash-outs, both of 'em. What makes people use their imagination so much? Some of them see a woman with fair hair they've never seen before, and can't get to the telephone fast enough."

He shrugged, almost lugubriously.

It was a five-minute drive to the magistrate's house, where it took ten minutes to get the search warrant signed by a fussy little man who asked a dozen questions, although he knew from the start that he would sign the warrant, and that the police wouldn't ask for it unless it was essential. Then they went back to the station. Just inside the charge room was Davis, standing and talking to the duty sergeant. Davis had a long, thin, pointed nose and sharp features – there was a certain briskness about his movements and intelligence in his eyes.

"Anything for me to do, sir?" he asked.

"Go and wait outside the house, will you?" said Roger. "And give a message to the sergeant who's watching it. Stop anyone going in, now, as well as anyone coming out."

"Yes, sir."

"Why that?" Carter asked, as Davis turned and hurried down the steps.

"Possible that some of Waite's voluntary workers will go there while he's out and do some envelope addressing," Roger answered briskly. "I'd rather no one knew when we got there."

"Fair enough. Let's go down to the canteen and have a beer," went on Carter; "won't be long before your chaps arrive. Want to know something?"

"Always willing to learn."

"What's changed you?" asked Carter, straight-faced, and he went on in the same tone: "Young Davis ought to go into the plain-clothes branch right away. He's done a damned good job on this case, although he's emotionally involved, as you might say. If a man can keep his emotions and this job separate—"

"What's this emotional involvement?"

"Didn't you know?" asked Carter. "Davis has been dating Atkinson's daughter Betty for several weeks. Pretty kid, no fool, either, Davis will be a lot of comfort to Mrs. A., too."

"Probably," said Roger, very thoughtfully. "How are the Atkinsons fixed financially?"

"Well, Mrs. A. will get a pension, so she won't have much to worry about. Wouldn't have, in any case, she had a tidy win on the pools a few years ago – that's how they came to buy the house they're in now. Picked up a cool ten thousand, I'm told."

Roger didn't speak, but a new thought sprang into his mind – new and devastating. Just after the Rawley case, Atkinson had acquired a small fortune.

So had another now dead witness – Mrs. Bray.

There were some suspicions, especially half-formed, that you didn't share with a Divisional man; notions which were better kept to oneself or to a select few.

This was one.

There was little he could do until morning, anyhow.

Carter led Roger into a small, modern canteen, bright with fluorescent lighting. Half a dozen men were there, two playing darts, two playing shove ha'penny. Glances which came Roger's way showed that he was recognised on sight. Carter went up to the bar and ordered two light ales.

"Lot of feeling here about Atkinson," he said. "Although the chaps don't show it much, they hate this killer's guts. But Parson Pete? Goddammit, half the chaps think he's a damned sight nearer right than wrong, if he'd only tone his arguments down a bit. If they find that he—"

"Know him well?" asked Roger,

"Fairly."

"How often does he get so worked up that he starts spluttering and looking like a dervish?"

"Know what you mean," said Carter. "When he starts spluttering, it's a bad sign, you wonder if he's all there. I haven't seen him like that for some time, I'd say he's quietening down a bit."

"Do you know how long he's known a Miss June Akers?"

"Didn't know he did. Atkinson might have known, but—" Carter quaffed his beer. "Why?"

"She doesn't seem to fit in with the leader of a little group of cranks."

"You'd be surprised the kind of people Peter Waite gets to help him at times," said Carter, dryly. "People who've just lost someone in a road accident, or had someone hurt, say. They feel so bitter, and Waite's campaign seems just the thing. Then they cool off – either his manner puts them off, or else it's just the way things are, they don't feel so hurt any more, and that's that. Callous lot of so-and-so's, we human beings."

"Profundity from Alfie Carter," said Roger, with a grin. "When I'm gone, try to find out if anyone here knows how long the Akers girl has known Waite, will you?"

"She got nice legs?"

"She's got nice everything."

"Proper lecher, that's what you are," Carter said, and finished his beer. " 'Nother one?"

"No, thanks," Roger said. "I'll go upstairs and find out if my chaps have arrived." They went up together, watched covertly by all the men present, and as they reached the hall a car drew up outside and two men got out – detective sergeants from the Yard, named Willis and Crew. Willis was tall, thin, pale-faced, Crew was a younger man, barely five feet eight. He was the photographer.

It took only a few minutes to brief them.

"Well, good luck," Carter said. "Don't photograph any of those posters of Waite's, though, none deserves to go down to posterity."

"I'll go ahead," Roger said to the Yard men as they reached the street. "You follow and park just behind me, and we'll go to the house all together. I'll have a word with the sergeant on duty there."

"Right, sir," said Willis.

It seemed darker as they neared the common; the lighting wasn't anything like good enough. Not dreaming that he was thinking almost exactly the same thing as Atkinson had, a few minutes before his death, Roger saw the dark outline of the houses as he got out of his car. He walked, making little sound with his rubber soles and heels, towards the spot where the sergeant was watching the house.

"Anyone gone in?"

"One man, just before I got your message from Constable Davis, sir. He's still inside."

"Thanks. Where's Davis?"

"In the grounds, sir."

"Thanks," said Roger again.

Davis was hidden against the background of the trees, invisible until the moment when he wanted to reveal himself. There was nothing he would like better than to come on the job with Roger; but it wouldn't be wise to favour him too much.

"Just stand by," Roger said, "and warn us if there's any sign of trouble."

"Yes, sir."

Roger went back to the Yard men, who were by their car but he didn't move on at once; the thing he had learned at the station was still nagging him.

"Won't be a minute," he said, and walked back to a telephone kiosk at a corner, stepped in, and called the Yard. He spoke to the Superintendent in charge, one Richard Reed.

"Dick, I think we ought to find out more about where Sergeant Atkinson's wife got her money from, just before Atkinson left Ligate," he said. "Will you contact Ligate, and find out which football pool she was supposed to have won, and everything possible about it."

"Right away," said Reed. "What's on?"

"Just a thought. If the pools win was all true, I'll forget it. If there's any doubt about it, I'd like to know."

"Supposing there's doubt?"

"We'd better check all the pools organisers, the earlier the better. But don't spread it about too much."

"All right, Handsome," Reed said. "If the Ligate night boys don't know, I'll talk to Jem Connolly."

"Fine," Roger said.

He went back to the waiting Yard men, in the quiet evening.

It seemed very dark, in spite of the faintly yellow light which showed just inside the hall. He didn't need an expert, for the door opened at a turn of the handle. The big hall seemed empty even when all three were inside it. It was strangely quiet as they walked up the stairs, Roger still in the lead. Radio music was coming from a downstairs room, but no door opened.

Half-way up the first flight of stairs, Roger sniffed.

"Burning, sir, isn't it?" tall Willis asked, wrinkling his nostrils. "Smell's like petrol, too."

"That's petrol all right," said Crew, hoisting up his camera.

Roger broke into a run on the landing, and raced up to Parson Pete's apartment.

The smell of burning and of petrol seemed much stronger, but there was no sign of smoke, no sign nor sound of fire. He put his shoulder to the door and heaved, but it was too stout to yield. He took a picklock out of his pocket, and with the tall and the short man standing just behind him, bent down and inserted the key, forcing himself to work it calmly and without rushing it. He felt the lock turn; if it slipped now he would have to start all over again.

There was no doubt that the burning was coming from the flat.

The lock clicked.

"Got it," Crew muttered.

Roger turned the handle and thrust the door open. It was like opening the door of a furnace. A fierce red glow shone just in front of him, he could see fire raging in the big campaign room. Smoke was billowing about, and seemed to be drawn out of a window which stood wide open. Was there a fire-escape just outside it?

The drawers of the filing-cabinet were wide open, and some papers were strewn about. The room at Mrs. Kitt's house must have looked something like this when the fire had started, but this was much more dangerous.

Smoke nearly smothered them as the door opened.

Crew began to cough.

"Phone—fire service," Roger said gaspingly. "Get—fire extinguishers." He saw the others turn and hurry downstairs, then went nearer the burning room; but the flames were fierce on his face, already close enough to sting. The records which he had come to photograph were blazing, there was little doubt that petrol had been poured on, and they had been set alight.

He couldn't do a thing with his hands. If there was a fire extinguisher in the flat it might help to salvage something. None of the other rooms was affected yet. He didn't think there was any hope of finding a fire extinguisher, but he had to try.

He saw the kitchen, the sink, the glittering taps and some tiles, through a door which was partly open. He pushed the door wider and stepped through, and as he did so, a man leapt at him from behind the door, a weapon raised high.

*An axe.*

## Chapter Fifteen

## Precious Records

Roger first saw the man when the axe was raised head high, and smashing down towards him. A split second later, he would have had no chance at all. Fear sliced through him as if the blade actually carved his head. If he turned to strike at the man, it couldn't miss him. He jumped forward desperately, seeing the shimmering blade as it swept down.

The man who was wielding it staggered.

There was no time for thought, only for swift impressions and reflex actions. One impression was vivid: that the axe was too heavy for the man, and the power he had put into the blow had carried him off balance. The axe struck the floor and a corner of the blade buried itself in as the man went staggering towards the door.

Roger pirouetted round.

He saw the little man. He saw the glitter in the dark eyes. He saw the pale face. It seemed to him that this man matched all the descriptions that he had heard – small, dark-clad, wearing a nearly black trilby, with a snub nose and glittering eyes, looking sideways.

Roger went for him.

The man didn't try to fight, but flung himself towards the door. He had a two yards' start, and moved very quickly. As he went through the doorway he thrust out a hand, caught the edge of the door and pushed it into Roger's face. It didn't swing fast, but fast enough to impede Roger and to lose him another yard. When he reached the tiny hallway, the man was at the open front door, with a hand on the side.

The roaring of the flames drowned every sound.

Smoke, thick and black, was swirling about the little hallway and the landing, tinged with the ugly red of fire. The snub-nosed man got outside, and this time slammed the door before Roger could reach it. The sudden draught took the smoke and the flame in the other direction, through the open window, and for a moment it was practically clear near Roger.

He snatched at the door knob, and pushed, and the door opened. The fresh draught brought more smoke and flame, but made no immediate difference. He couldn't see the fugitive but could hear his footsteps clattering down the stairs. Roger reached the top flight, put a hand on the banister rail, and jumped. He reached a half landing only two yards behind the man, who sensed the imminence of danger, and swung round.

Roger didn't stop.

They crashed into one another, Roger's weight so much greater than the other's that they toppled downwards, Roger on top. He could do nothing to ease the force of the fall. In the last split second, he knew that nothing could stop the back of the man's head from smashing against the landing.

The thud was sickening.

Roger felt the man go limp as he turned to take his own weight on his shoulder. He rolled clear, but the other did not move, simply lay there with his face turned towards the wall, his eyes closed, his legs on the bottom stairs. Dazedly, Roger got to his feet. He stared down at the little man, and saw the blood oozing sluggishly from the wound – blood, as quickly as this. He felt the smoke at his eyes, and could hardly breathe because he was so out of breath. And he couldn't do a thing.

He shouldn't do a thing.

A doctor—

Then he heard a man call out: "You all right, sir?" Who was that? A man came hurrying, he could hear his footsteps, followed by the insistent: "You all right, sir?"

It was Davis.

"Send for—police-surgeon," Roger said, articulating very slowly and carefully. "Ambulance, too. Hurry."

"Are *you* all right?"

"Yes. Hurry, I said."

"Yes, sir." There was a red glow on Davis's eyes and pale face, for the door was open at Parson Pete's flat. Roger looked up. Flames were showing at the doorway, black smoke came out suddenly as if caught by a stiffening wind. Roger started up the stairs, holding tightly to the banister rail because he wasn't yet steady, but he knew that it was a waste of time.

All of those records were gone.

Half-way up the stairs, Roger stopped, said *"Fool!"* and returned to the unconscious man. He didn't like what he remembered of the sound of the thud of his head, and he liked less the pool of blood, growing bigger and bigger as it oozed from the cracked skull. At least he could check that bleeding.

As he bent down, he saw a little white powder near the man's coat, obviously spilt from the pocket. It was very fine and floury. Roger almost forgot the man in that moment. Here, coming so swiftly that there was hardly time to think, was a discovery which might alter his whole outlook on the case. With great deliberation he damped his finger on the powder, and then put it to his tongue.

"It is," he said aloud. "It's snow."

There were several packets of opium in the injured man's pockets.

And Charles Jackson had drawn up the report of the Government Committee on Dangerous Drugs.

Willis and Crew arrived with fire extinguishers, and a fire service crew soon followed. There was no hope yet of getting into the Campaign room, and Roger would only get in the way of the firemen. He went down to the next landing.

A doctor had arrived, closely followed by an ambulance. Next, Davis.

"I radioed from your car, sir, hope that was right."

"Damned right it was," Roger said. He found himself offering Davis a cigarette as he watched the doctor and the ambulance men bending over the still, pale figure. The opium was now in his own pocket, like a leaden weight. "I hope to heaven I didn't kill him."

"Better that than if he'd killed you, sir." Davis was watching the scene intently. "I've seen him about several times, seen him come here, too. If you asked me, I'd say he was one of Mr. Waite's campaign helpers."

"That's what I'm afraid of."

"Went berserk, did he?" asked Davis, and then went on in that matter-of-fact way of his: "I wonder what makes a man go like that, sir?"

"I know what could," Roger said, but he didn't explain. Opium, or the lack of it, could make an addict behave like Waite. "I wonder what else there was in those files and in that Campaign room." He started up the stairs, but realised even before he reached Waite's landing that there wasn't a chance of getting inside. Three firemen and their snaking hoses were at the top of the stairs, spraying water on to the rooms. Other firemen were outside, at the back. The Chief Officer, elderly and greying, looked round impatiently.

"We haven't enough room as it is."

"Salvage everything you can from that big room," Roger urged. "I won't get in your way, but salvage everything."

"We'll be lucky even if we stop the fire from spreading; there won't be anything left in *that* room," the man said.

At ten o'clock Roger stepped out of his car and into Divisional Headquarters, the wind cutting along the street making him shiver; it was colder tonight than it had been for weeks, and pitch dark with it.

He saw the time by the police-station clock.

In the Granada, Waite and the girl were still sitting watching the film. Unsuspecting? It was pointless to guess.

They had driven straight to a car-park behind the cinema, Davis had reported, and then gone straight to the cinema and bought their tickets, so there was nothing to suggest that they had passed on any message. But – why had the man gone to the flat to destroy the records? Why had he chosen the very hour that Roger had visited Waite?

Coincidence? Again?

Once Waite and June Akers had gone into the cinema, Davis had returned to the H.Q., calling on Betty Atkinson on the way, but that hadn't delayed him many minutes. Inside the Granada, however, there were telephones, and Waite or the girl could have telephoned a message to the snub-nosed man.

Davis was back at the cinema, finding out from the doorman and the cashier whether Waite and June Akers had gone straight into the auditorium, or whether either of them had used a telephone. Davis would wait until the show was over, and a man was to follow them. They might go back to the house, or Waite might see the girl home.

Another detective would be standing by to telephone directly the theatre emptied; Roger intended to go back to the wrecked apartment in time to see Waite's reaction for himself.

Carter was up in the little office, still in a haze of smoke, with his tie undone and the ends hanging down, red-faced and matter-of-fact as ever.

"What you want is a wash and brush up, you look like the original chimney sweep out of the Water Babies," he greeted. "Got some stuff for you, though, we'll show you how quick a Division can work when it wants to. This June Akers – you wouldn't happen to be aware of her relationship to another Certain Person Involved, would you?"

"She's Mrs. Kitt's niece, if that's what you mean."

Carter's face dropped.

"Oh, lor'," he said, "one of the chief troubles is that you're sometimes nearly as good as your reputation. That's right, she is Mrs. Kitt's niece. Matter of fact, that's how it is I can tell you anything about her. One of our chaps was over at Ligate until a couple of years ago, he recognised June Akers, and last week she and the parson were seen together in Totting High Street. My chap talked about it in the canteen. The story didn't reach me, I *never* gossip, but several of the chaps knew. That's item one. Item two –

there's a bundle of stuff over from Ligate. Documents on that Rawley case, as far as I can make out, photographs, all that kind of thing. Want it now?"

"Please."

"That wash and—"

"Cleanliness can wait," Roger said, and took out the packet he had taken from the injured man's pocket. He felt a tension greater than any he had known since the start of the case, for this opened a new, almost frightening vista. "Have a taste," he said.

Carter frowned. "What's that?"

"Snow."

"My Gawd! *All* of it?"

"I'd say so," said Roger.

"Found at *Waite's* place?"

"Found on a man trying to get away from Waite's place,"

Roger said. "Send it to the Yard by special messenger, will you? The sooner we know all about it, the better."

"Will I," breathed Carter.

Roger handed the packet over, then sat at the empty desk and took out the Rawley case documents. They didn't miss much. Here were photographs, police drawings and diagrams showing the scene of the accident, medical reports, newspaper clippings and – the bulkiest of them all – the record, in almost copperplate handwriting, of everything that had been said in court. Here was the statement of every witness, both for the defence and for the prosecution. There was even a verbatim report of Mrs. Kitt's pungent statement, that the case should never have been brought and she could not understand what the police were doing to waste public money in such a way; it was written down without comment.

There were several photographs of the woman victim – one, as she lay on the ground just after the accident, and the nose of the Jaguar was there, together with a man climbing out of it. For the rest, the picture was all feet of people hurrying to the spot. There were two portrait photographs of Mary Rawley, and she looked exactly what she had been described as – comely, placid and pleasant-faced, rather like Peter Waite's mother.

There was a full-length photograph of the driver of the Jaguar. He was a heavy jowled, bulky-looking man with wide-set eye – not a man to take to from his photograph, probably a middle-aged business-man, possibly very prosperous. His evidence had been clear and straightforward, and a reading of the other statements made it quite clear that in dismissing the case, the magistrates had taken the only possible course.

"How're you doing?" Carter asked, as he came into the office.

"Fair," said Roger, gruffly. "Mrs. Bray, defence witness. Atkinson, defence witness – Jackson called him, and he had to go in the box. Jackson, defence lawyer. Mrs. Kitt, the magistrate who approved the decision. Nearly a clean sweep. Alf, get on to the Yard for me. Have them get in touch with Benjamin Cunliffe – the driver of this Jaguar." He tapped the photograph. "Everyone else connected with the defence of that motorist has been victimised in some way or other, he might be next on the list. I'll go over and see him as soon as I'm through with this, but we want him protected. We also want to make absolutely sure that Charles Jackson is all right." Carter was already lifting the telephone.

"What's on your mind, Handsome? Think this Watch Committee of Waite's decided—" He stopped. "Oh, gawd, no," he breathed, and then spoke into the telephone: "Gimme Dick Reed." He held on again. "Think Waite *is* mad?" he demanded. "Maybe a dopey?"

"Someone's mad. Someone's desperate, too, and meant to make sure we didn't search that apartment. It could have been because of the snow, but it might also be because of the Campaign records. Good thing I took down the names and current addresses of all the members of the Watch Committee, and that includes Rawley, the husband of the woman who died. Another thing, Alf. Their first job was Mrs. Bray, killed three months or so ago on a zebra crossing. She worked for a family named Marsden, and was looking after a youngster. She pushed the kid to safety, but—well, check that the Marsdens aren't associated with Parson Pete, will you?"

"I'll pass that on, yes—hallo, Dick! Alf here, got a week's work for you from Handsome West."

He seemed to forget that Roger was present, and was still talking briskly when there was a tap at the door, and a uniformed constable put his head inside the room.

"Mr. West, sir, there's a message for you – the Granada show's over, they're coming out."

"Fine," said Roger. "Thanks."

He mouthed a message to Carter, who waved him away, and then hurried downstairs. His car was pointing in the right direction. He had forgotten the mess that he was in, and was intent only on seeing the effect of the fire on Waite and on June Akers.

Near the dark Fields, cars were clustered, the inevitable crowd of sightseers had gathered opposite the burned house, but there wasn't much to see from here. Firemen were rolling up their hoses, and one engine had gone. A police sergeant came up to report that several firemen were still inside the flat, that the fire had been confined to the one apartment, and only the big room had been gutted – *so* badly that the roof had caved in at one corner, and the floor wasn't safe.

"Not much chance of getting anything out, sir."

"That's bad," said Roger, and then heard the stutter of a motor cycle, and looked along the road. It was Davis, as he had half-expected; Davis had a remarkable knack of turning up just when he was wanted. He pulled up alongside, and said in a quiet voice: "They went straight into the auditorium, sir, that's quite certain."

"Did you ask if they'd come out at all, for the toilet, say, or—"

"Made sure that the telephone was only used twice after they went in, once by an usherette, and once by someone who came in from the street," Davis said. "It's in full view of the cash desk and the doorman, they're both quite sure about it. The cashier goes off at nine o'clock, and we know the chap broke into the apartment before then, so two people can swear that Waite and the girl didn't telephone anybody."

"Yes, pretty conclusive," Roger said. "Thanks."

Two or three cars came along slowly, drivers and passengers curious and puzzled. Another car turned the corner, and stopped. A policeman spoke to the driver, and even at a distance Roger could see that it was a woman.

He walked quickly towards the car – June Akers' Hillman.

He heard Waite saying something. Then Waite got out on one side and the girl the other. In the full light of a street-lamp, they stared at the top of the house, the girl with a hand on Waite's arm, Waite with an expression of bewilderment and dismay.

It was never possible to be sure, but it seemed to Roger that the man was not only surprised but astounded.

Then Waite exclaimed, "My records, my precious records!" and he made a rush towards the house.

"Peter!" June Akers cried, and moved swiftly after him. "Peter, come back!"

Roger let them go; and followed.

## Chapter Sixteen

# Despair?

The Reverend Peter Waite stood on the landing outside his flat and stared at the wreckage inside. Water had made as much mess as the fire. The whole landing, as well as the little hallway and the entrance to the Campaign room, was a litter of burned paper, burnt wood and water – or rather black, soggy mud. Big footprints led to the kitchen, too, but Waite did not glance that way, he looked only into the big room.

The girl stood with a hand on his arm.

A fireman was by his side, as if ready to stop him if he tried to go in.

Waite had lost all his colour; in fact, his face had a greyish, pasty look, and there was a sheen as of perspiration on it. His eyes seemed filled with horror. His mouth was open, his teeth parted.

Just within sight was what remained of the steel filing-cabinet. So fierce had been the heat that part of it seemed to have melted, and it had lost its shape. All the drawers stood open, and inside there was only a charred mass of papers; probably there wasn't a decipherable record left. The cabinet was sinking into the floor at one side, and floor-boards and joists showed through to the ceiling of the room below.

"Everything," Waite said, in a low-pitched, hoarse voice. "Everything."

"Peter—" the girl began.

"Ten years' work," he continued, as if she hadn't spoken. "Ten whole years, and everything is destroyed, even the records of those who would try to help. Everything. His gaze roamed towards the posters on the walls – most of them charred and unrecognisable, all curling away from the wall like old wallpaper. Some of those at the top had been only scorched, and the colours still showed brightly.

"Ten—years—work," he repeated, in that broken voice, and his shoulders seemed to sag. "It's almost as if God is against me."

In turning to put a hand on his shoulder, as if she hoped that her touch would help Waite, who was fighting for his self- control, June Akers saw Roger. She hadn't noticed him before. She didn't speak, but made no attempt to look away; there was a kind of defiance in her manner.

Roger spoke to the fireman.

"We want the remains of that cabinet badly, what are the chances of getting it?"

"Daresay we can, if it's really urgent."

"It's vital. And the typewriter, too?"

"We got that out," the fire officer said. "It's downstairs with some of the other stuff salvaged from the other rooms. Seeing what a hold the fire had got when we arrived, we didn't do so badly."

"No one suggested you did," Roger said quickly. "First-class job." It had been. He watched the fireman beckon others, and moved aside as they went cautiously into the room to get the filing-cabinet. He looked at June Akers. "Do you know if Mr. Waite has any neighbours he can stay the night with, Miss Akers?"

"He can come home with me," the girl said. "I've plenty of room."

"People might misunderstand—"

"I don't care what people think." She didn't flare up; just said that evenly, but perhaps with quiet anger.

"Mr. Waite might care," said Roger, dryly.

"It's time something happened to make him think more about himself and less about others," June Akers said sharply. "He's practically crucified himself. Why, he—"

"Why don't you drive over to your aunt's house, at Ligate?" Roger suggested. "There's plenty of room there, your uncle and an aunt are staying there, too, so you won't invite any hurtful gossip for Mr. Waite, but you'll still be able to keep an eye on him."

She was obviously surprised by the revelation that he knew that she was Mrs. Kitt's niece. Waite had taken no notice of them, but seemed shocked to numbness by the scene of destruction. He turned away from it now, however, his hands clenched, his eyes glittering.

"I'll send a man over with you," Roger promised the girl.

"I can manage quite well." The girl was sharp.

"I'm sure you can. But I'll send a man with you, and I'll come myself as soon as I can. I'd like a word with you." He smiled while waiting for her to argue, but she didn't, just turned to Waite and held out her hand. Holding hands, they went downstairs.

Roger went into the flat. The firemen had already lifted the cabinet to a safer patch of the floor. Soon they had it in the next room, which had been hardly damaged, although there was a big hole in one wall.

Roger hurried downstairs, told Willis to go in the car with the girl and Waite, and Crew to follow them.

He was back in the bedroom, studying the cabinet with the fire officer and two men, when he heard heavy footsteps, and looked round to see Carter coming in. Carter was monstrous in a double-breasted suit of brown tweed, and his chins quivered. The firemen were lifting the charred wreckage out of the cabinet and putting it in cardboard boxes, but there seemed nothing that could be salvaged at all; certainly none of the record cards had survived.

"Did a job of it, didn't they?" remarked Carter.

He would only have come in real emergency.

"Not bad. What got you out of your chair?"

"Something dam' queer, Handsome; thought I'd come and see you myself. This chap Cunliffe, the driver of the Jaguar. His wife is a dopey."

Roger didn't speak, just stood and let the night's discoveries sink in. Dope in a man's pocket, dope perhaps in Waite's room, and now this.

"How long's she been addicted?" Roger asked at last.

"Been like it a year or more," Carter said. "Chap's had a hell of a time. How about that?"

Roger said very slowly, "What dope?"

"Heroin."

"Anyone know where she gets it?"

"No. She's had two cures, in for another now."

"Anything else known?"

"No."

"Where's Cunliffe?"

"At his home in Regent's Park. The place is being watched, but I haven't tried to get in touch with him. I talked to Micky Smith over at St. John's Wood; he knew the case history. He says that Cunliffe's wife started mixing with a fast set a few years ago, and she probably got the dope from them, but he's never been able to make sure. She always says it was first given to her by strangers. The usual story – a little shot or two to begin with, pleasant dreams, and then – it's cost her a fortune, too. Cunlilfe a fortune, I mean."

"So there isn't one of the defence witnesses in the Rawley case who hasn't suffered some kind of hell," Roger said tautly. "Thanks, Alf. Anything from the hospital about that man with the broken skull?"

"Unconscious. No change."

Roger found himself lighting a cigarette. Thoughts were whirling in his mind, he had hardly considered one before another drove it out.

*All* of the defence had suffered, and that couldn't be anything but by design.

"Get anything on Rawley himself?" Roger asked.

"So far, not a thing," said Carter. "He moved from Ligate soon after his wife died, that's about all. I asked the Yard to trace him. But surely a man wouldn't—"

"We don't know, do we?" Roger said roughly, and then stared at the firemen. Practically all the charred paper was out of the filing-cabinet. It was so burned that much of it powdered at a touch, and he didn't think there was any hope of getting a thing from it; at least he'd tried. He went closer to look, and saw a fireman staring at the back of one of the top drawers, as if at something he didn't understand. It was so buckled that to Roger there was nothing surprising in anything that might be found at the bottom.

"Something's melted," the fireman said. "Metal of some kind—lead, I'd say. Wasn't only paper kept in here, that's for sure." He poked about with a screwdriver. "Powder, too."

Carter ejaculated, *"Powder?"*

"S'right."

"Let me have a look," Roger said, and when he stared at the powder which was on the edge of the screwdriver, he took a little off with his finger-nail. He sniffed, but all he could get was the strong odour of burning.

"Not the same, but let's get that analysed, quick," he said. "Have a report telephoned to me at Mrs. Kin's house, Alf, will you? I'm on my way there. If that's what I think it is—"

"I know who you'll put in a cell to cool his heels," Carter said.

Roger drove alone through the gloomy streets of London's suburbs. Shop windows were nearly all in darkness, and street-lamps did little to break the gloom. He went along the main streets much of the way, through the thin midnight traffic; only here and there did he pass a bus. He kept flicking on his radio, for news from the Yard or from the car which was following Waite and June Akers. He contacted it three times; everything was normal. Waite had stopped in the car outside the girl's flat, in Clapham, while she had gone in for a night-case; that was the only stop, and they were now in Ligate and would soon be at Mrs. Kitt's house.

There was no further word about the unconscious fire-raiser.

Roger was near the Ligate borough border when his radio crackled, and he heard the familiar call: "Calling Chief Inspector

West, calling Chief Inspector West." It was like a refrain. "Can you hear me?"

"West speaking, can you hear me?"

"Yes, sir, message for you from Mr. Evans, in the laboratory. First powder sent is opium, one hundred per cent, the second is heroin, eighty-five per cent, fifteen per cent French chalk. Message ends. That's the lot, sir, did you get it?"

"Yes, I got it," Roger said, "thanks. Over to you."

He flicked the lever.

Things in this case seemed to have been done by madmen, and heroin and opium could drive men to the borderline of insanity, the craving for it could turn them mad.

He put his foot down harder.

He knew Ligate well, reached the Broadway and then turned towards the Heath. Was it odd that both Mrs. Kitt and Waite should live in houses near open land, and which were much alike in period and size? At least he could put that down to coincidence.

Couldn't he?

He turned into the road which led to Mrs. Kitt's. He saw the corner, round which the observant P.C. Pye had come, noticing the Iso. The house was less dark than usual, and several lights were on.

He turned a corner.

He saw three things.

First, a car standing just beyond the gates of Mrs. Kitt's house, with its sidelights on. The light of a street-lamp shone in such a way that he could just make out the figure of the driver.

Second, Peter Waite, turning out of the driveway, as if blindly.

Third, a policeman on the other side of the road, and running into the road.

Then, the engine of the car roared, and the car leapt forward.

## Chapter Seventeen

# Near Miss

Waite was no more than ten yards away from Roger, the other car was ten yards farther on. The roar of the engine was like that of a swooping aircraft. Hearing it, Waite spun round as if tugged by the actual sound, and he stood for a split second on the pavement, his arms held outwards and upwards, one foot in front of the other. He did not move, it was almost as if he welcomed the killer car.

The policeman flung himself at the car, as if he believed he could push it out of the way. He reached the door, grabbed the handle and clung on, while Waite stood there waiting, all in that split second of time, when life and death seemed to be part of each other.

Roger jammed his thumb on the horn.

It blared out above the noise of the car engine. He flicked his headlights on, and they shone right into the face of the driver. He saw the way the policeman was being dragged along, saw the front wheels of the car turned towards the pavement and the waiting man.

The wheels were only two yards away from Waite.

The driver wrenched the wheel, and the car changed direction. Its nearside wheel mounted the kerb, bumped up, then thumped down again. It gathered speed. Waite went flying, the constable ran alongside the car desperately trying to open the door and get at the driver. Roger trod on his brakes. The other car was heading for him one moment, the next it was almost at right-angles to him. The policeman was out of sight. Roger turned his wheel to try to collide into the other car broadside on, but the man swung his wheel again. There was a sharp rending sound, of bumper on to a wing, then the other car surged forward. Roger caught a glimpse of the policeman staggering in the road, and the car's red lights fading; then he pulled up on the grass verge of the Heath, switching the radio on.

"Calling all cars, calling all cars. Chief Inspector West speaking from Ligate Heath Road, Ligate Heath Road. All cars converge on Ligate to stop Morris car, black or dark blue, with damaged right wing. Please pass message on – over."

"Message received," a man said, "message being passed on, all cars to converge on Ligate Heath Road …"

Roger flicked the radio off and slid out of the car. The policeman wasn't hurt, and had recovered himself and was hurrying across towards Waite. Waite was in a crumpled heap on the pavement close to the wall of Mrs. Kitt's house, and all Roger could see were his feet, his legs, back and the back of his head; his arms were folded beneath him.

Roger watched the policeman go down on one knee, reach underneath Waite's body for his hand. He straightened the man a little and then felt his pulse.

"How is he?" Roger asked quietly.

"Seems okay, sir—knocked out, I think, he hit the wall I should say."

"Probably." Roger recognised P. C. Pye; if nothing else, this case was bringing out some first-class men from the ranks. "Think he needs a doctor?"

"Doubt it, sir."

"Good." In the distance Roger could hear engines roaring, and wondered whether the patrol cars would get the fugitive Morris, or whether the driver was good enough to run the gauntlet and get away. He heard nearby sounds, first of a door opening, so that light streamed out, then the running footsteps of a woman. He wondered what had happened to Willis and Crew, but didn't ask Pye. He went towards the gate and saw June Akers running swiftly, a dark silhouette against the bright light.

"Is Peter all right?" she called sharply.

"Knocked out, I think."

"I heard a crash," she began, then pushed past Roger towards Waite. She knelt down, as Pye had done, and felt his pulse. Pye had eased him over on his side, so that the lamplight fell on his face, showing the pallor, the bruise and slight bleeding at the forehead. The girl didn't lose her head, and gave Roger an impression of great competence as she looked up at Pye and said, "Will you help me carry him into the house?"

"I'll carry him, miss," Pye said reassuringly, and hoisted Waite up as easily as he would a child. June followed, and Roger went with her, studying her set profile, the lift of her chin, the way she walked.

"What made him come out?" he asked.

"He had a telephone message."

"Do you know who it was from?"

"He didn't say. He just put the phone down and said he had to go and meet someone. That car must have been waiting for him."

"Yes. To kill."

"It's hideous," June said. "And Peter—" She didn't finish.

"Wanted to do away with himself, didn't he?" Roger asked dryly.

She didn't answer, but quickened her pace and led the way into a large room, opposite the one where Mrs. Kitt had been attacked. She put on the light. Pye carried Waite across to an old-fashioned sofa; the whole room looked as if it had been furnished sixty years earlier, and nothing had been altered. By then Waite was beginning to stir.

"Shall I give him a spot of brandy, sir, or—" Pye touched his hip pocket.

"Let him come round by himself," Roger advised. "Didn't two men come here with him and Miss Akers?"

"Yes, sir," Pye said, "but there was a message for them from the Yard. They went back, sir, and two others are on their way from the Division. I said I could look after things for the interval."

"Heaven knows you tried. Feel all right?"

"Yes, sir, thanks."

"Hurt?"

"Just grazed my knuckles and knee a bit."

"Well, patch yourself up if you need it, and stay at the front door and see that I'm not bothered for a bit, will you?"

"Certainly, sir."

Pye went out, closing the door as he went. June Akers stood by the head of the sofa, first staring down on Waite, then pressing her hand against her forehead, and looking up at Roger. Her clear eyes were glassy, as if the night's shocks were catching up with her and she had a vicious headache.

"What happened when you got here?" Roger asked abruptly.

"Well—nothing really," she said rather drearily. "Peter was terribly upset. He's been living on his nerves for a long time, and I know he's not even having enough to eat – he gives away too much of his stipend, and spends far too much on the Campaign. I don't think you could imagine what a terrible blow it was when he found everything destroyed. *Everything.*" She uttered the word much as Waite had done when he had looked at the soaking mess in his Campaign room.

"What exactly do you mean by everything?" Roger asked.

"Please don't ask pointless questions," she said. "All he's worked for for ten years—"

"The safety campaign?"

"Of course. What else?"

Roger said dryly, "That's what I'm wondering. Earlier this evening he'd told me he was on the point of giving the Campaign up altogether. He knew that most of the people helping him had lost any enthusiasm they ever had. Why should the loss of a few names and addresses of people no longer interested affect him so much?"

She said, slowly, "He'd never have given it up. And the shock"

"Think it was just the shock?" Roger asked brusquely. "What else was in that Campaign room cabinet?"

She didn't answer.

But she drew a deep breath, and obviously the question both hurt and shook her. She looked down at Waite, whose eyelids were flickering and who moved his arms a little.

"Well, what was in it?" Roger was hard-voiced.

She would not look at him, and she would not answer. She knew the answer all right. She stood tall and slim, eyes clear in spite of their burning, with a kind of pride and a wholesomeness which it seemed hard to believe was really corrupt.

"What—?" he began.

"You can't harass him—" the girl protested.

"I want to see what he has to say," Roger said roughly. "Waite, listen to me." His voice made Waite open his eyes wide, as if startled. "Waite, what else was in that cabinet?"

Waite said, "Why didn't you let me die?"

*"What else was in that cabinet?"*

Waite's eyes widened, and he closed his mouth tightly, as if he felt some new threat. The girl gripped Roger's shoulders.

"You can't torment him now. You—"

"If you interfere, I'll have you held on a charge," Roger said coldly. "Keep quiet, please. Waite, what else was in that cabinet?"

There was a long pause. Then: "Everything," Waite said at last, "everything. Hope and faith—everything. Everyone who would help – I don't even know where to write to them now, I lost everything."

*"What else was in that cabinet?"*

"Everything," the man repeated, and it was like a sigh.

"Don't pretend you're ill, answer me. There was a powder in that cabinet. What was it?"

"Powder?" echoed Waite, and his gaze steadied and he seemed to be trying to understand and to answer. "Powder? *Powder and shot!*" He flinched. "Powder—" His eyes widened, and there was something in his expression which it was hard to understand. "Powder," he repeated. "French chalk, we—" He gulped. "We had socials. Get everyone to work all the time. All work and no play makes Jack a dull boy. Those dances. French chalk," he went on, much more clearly, "but what does it matter? French chalk, to put on the floor to make it slippery so that the workers could dance."

June said, with a catch in her breath, "He doesn't *know*." Roger straightened up, very slowly.

"But you do," he said.

"I've nothing to say," said Councillor Mrs. Kitt's niece. "There is nothing I can tell you."

She would not say another word.

"All right," said Roger, when more men from the Division had arrived, "we'll take Miss Akers to the Yard until she's willing to talk. We'd better take Waite, too, he may not be such a fool as he's making out." He was in the room where Mrs. Kitt had been attacked, with three local C.I.D. men. He was on edge to get back to the Yard, to be able to call on any man he needed, with specialists of all kinds at hand. There were limits to what the Divisions could do, and when two Divisions as far apart as Ligate and Totting were concerned it was almost impossible to have proper liaison.

He wanted every man on Waite's original Watch Committee under surveillance and questioned about his activities tonight. He wanted the latest report on the little man whom he had jumped on at the staircase of Waite's place. He wanted to find out if Mrs. Kitt was able to talk yet, whether her husband could tell them anything more to help. Kitt was out, at the hospital with the sister who had come to visit him; a bad sign. There was Benjamin Cunliffe to see, about his wife, and a check with St. John's Wood about her access to the heroin. And he wanted to see Jackson again. Now there were two common factors – involvement in the old accident, and involvement in dangerous drugs.

And Roger wanted desperately to know how much more heroin there was about, and to find Rosemary Jackson. More than anything, Jackson's wife was on his mind.

She was still asleep, dreaming those wonderful dreams.

Roger sent Peter Waite and the girl to Scotland Yard under a Divisional escort, and drove to St. John's Wood, where the Night Duty Inspector gave him more details about Mrs. Cunliffe's drug addiction.

"It's a miserable case," the Inspector said. "Cunliffe dotes on the woman. She's fifteen years younger than he is and quite something to look at. Every now and again she goes on a kind of heroin binge, you know what that's like. She comes back with a good supply, too. And because he knows how much she suffers when she doesn't get it, he lets her have it for a week or two. Then he faces the fact that it can't go on, and reports it again, and she's sent for another cure. I've known Cunliffe for ten years," the D.I. went on, "and now he's married to a human wreck. Tragic, for a man like him."

"How far away does he live?" asked Roger, "and where's his wife?"

"She's in a home, but they kid themselves over these cures," the D.I. said cynically. "I talked to Cunliffe when I had the message from Totting. He said he'd be up until the small hours, and would be glad to see you if you wanted to call. Not that he thinks he can help."

It was nearly one o'clock.

"Sure this isn't too late to find him reasonable?" Roger asked.

"Not for Cunliffe," the D.I. said definitely. "How about taking me along?"

The driver of the car which had killed Mrs. Rawley nearly four years ago was still up and fully dressed.

Roger had only the four-year-old photograph to judge him from, and sight of the man in the flesh showed him to be vigorous, alert, much more of a personality than his picture suggested. The house near Regent's Park stood in its own grounds, and was quite beautiful in its simplicity of line. The immediate impression inside was of great wealth and excellent taste. Cunliffe looked tired, but the appearance of buoyant health and prosperity couldn't be missed.

"Yes," he said to Roger, briskly. "I sometimes think that it's retribution for that woman I killed, although to this day I don't think there was a thing I could do. It wasn't my fault at all. Unless I was going too fast, at twenty-five miles an hour, and sometimes—" He broke off. "It was as if a curse was laid upon me. A few months afterwards my wife fell ill, and I didn't realise at the time that it was drug addiction. When I found out—"

He broke off, shrugging his shoulders as he stood in front of the fireplace in a high, spacious Regency room, with dark-blue velvet curtains drawn, surrounded by all these evidences of wealth, and yet set in tragedy.

"I discovered what had happened a few weeks after she'd run away from me," he went on. "She was much younger than I, I feared there had been an *affaire,* but thought that if I was patient she would realise how silly she was. When she came back, she was ill. That was the beginning of it. She—" He caught his breath. "She always blamed me."

"For what?"

"She's always refused to say where she got the drugs, but said it was at one of the welfare committees she worked on. She did a lot of social work, because I urged her to—she simply hadn't enough to do here, and I thought it would do her good. Instead—"

"Which particular welfare committee?" Roger was sharp.

"I don't know."

"Was it the Peter Waite *Stop Murder on the Roads* Committee?"

"She served on that, but I don't know if it was where she got the heroin," Cunliffe insisted. "Everyone's tried to make her tell, even the staff at the Palli Clinic, where she has these so-called cures, but she's adamant. I think she's afraid that if she talks she'll never get the drug again."

"I see," Roger said, and took out a typewritten list, copied from the addresses he had taken from Waite's cabinet before the fire, and went on, "Do you recognise any of these names, Mr. Cunliffe?"

Cunliffe studied the list.

Roger watched him.

In the place of this man it would be easy to picture Charles Jackson, his eyes burning with the fear of despair. Charles Jackson – in love with his young, pretty wife who had disappeared.

Had that anything to do with his report on dangerous drugs?

## Chapter Eighteen

# Big Effort

"The only name that's familiar on this list is Arthur Rawley," Cunliffe said. "I haven't seen him since the trial. I wrote to him afterwards and asked if there was anything I could do – I didn't lack money, and he was poor. I didn't get a reply. There really wasn't anything else I could do. The fact of having the death of that woman on my conscience was bad enough, and I wished I could have got some response from the husband, but I could understand it, especially if he really thought I was responsible for her death. If anyone killed my wife—" He broke off.

Roger didn't interrupt.

"If I could find the people who first gave my wife this drug, if I knew who was supplying her now, I think I would kill them with my own hands," Cunliffe said with great deliberation.

"Have you no idea?"

"None."

"You say she goes to a home for a cure?"

"Yes, she's been to the Palli Clinic several times," said Cunliffe. "On the first two occasions it was all done privately, and the police weren't informed. I hoped it would be possible to cure her without making her feel that the police were watching her. As it was, her nervous condition—"

She must have given this man hell, Roger thought.

"This last occasion I've told the police, but they haven't yet been able to find out from where she obtained her supplies," Cunliffe said. "When she comes out she'll be closely watched, I've had to take that risk, but – Mr. West, my wife was a most beautiful woman. She was most generous, kindly and even-tempered. If you had watched the gradual change in her, as I did, and seen the hideous metamorphosis, you would have been appalled. It has affected not only her nerves, but also her looks and general health. Sometimes I wonder if it's really possible that she is the same woman."

There seemed nothing more to say, nothing more to do, tonight, so Roger said good night and left.

"What do you make of him?" the St. John's Wood man asked.

"He takes a bit of sizing up," Roger said cautiously. "What do you know about the Palli Clinic?"

"Damned expensive nursing home for neurotics and dopeys," said the other. "All right if you can afford it. There's a resident doctor, qualified nursing staff and a dozen consultants, a lot of them from Harley and Wimpole Streets. It's got a good reputation, and they have some pretty rough stuff to deal with at times. These dopeys go crazy, and—but who'm I talking to?"

"Me – thanks," Roger grinned. "Well, now I want to find out if Jackson's back home."

Jackson wasn't, and there was still no news of Rosemary Jackson. But there was a late report saying that Jackson hadn't left his wife's mother until nearly midnight.

Roger drove back to Divisional H.Q. but didn't get out of the car. It was then nearly one o'clock, and his eyes were stinging with tiredness which would get worse for a while, then probably ease until morning. He was in no mood to go back to an empty house, and try to sleep; he did want to see Jackson. A couple of stiff whiskies, and he would be as good as needs be. He drove fast through the almost deserted streets, and reached the Yard in little more than ten minutes. The big, red-brick civil police buildings were nearly in darkness, but plenty of lights showed at the windows of the Criminal Investigation Department building. He parked his car where there was plenty of room, walked past the police on duty and hurried up the steps, then up in the lift. He went first to his own office, which was empty and dark. He switched on the light. The fire was out, and it was chilly. The stale smell of tobacco smoke hung about the room, and he lit a cigarette. He went to his own desk, which was piled with reports and memoranda – there was a full two hours' work here, but this wasn't what he wanted to do at this time.

Then he remembered that he'd forgotten to telephone Janet, his wife, at ten o'clock.

She'd realise that he was busy, of course, but—

He caught his breath, in vexation.

The evening papers were full of the killer "accidents", his name was mentioned in them all, Janet would know what kind of a case he was on, and she would probably worry desperately. Why the hell hadn't he telephoned? He smiled reluctantly, remembering what he had been doing at ten o'clock. It was too late to call Janet now, but first thing in the morning was a "must".

He glanced through the memoranda, to find out if anything was urgent. Among the top ones was a pencilled note:

*Mrs. West telephoned at 11.40. I told her that you were at the Divisions.*

There was nothing else, except a picture of Arthur Rawley, as he had been at the time of his wife's death together with a biographical note. Rawley had been assistant manager of a small branch of a multiple chemists, was qualified pharmaceutically, and seemed to have been doing well; at the time he had been only twenty-seven. He looked meek and mild; one could imagine him offering advice to mothers with their babies, mixing National Health medicines, measuring the drugs—

Drugs.

Here was a third man involved in the four-year-old accident and, in some way, with dangerous drugs.

Roger read the rest of the report on Rawley quickly and hopefully – where did the man live now, where did he now work?

According to a report from Connolly of Ligate, Rawley had left the district soon after the loss of his wife. He was no longer on the staff of Smarts the Chemists, at any branch. He had no known relatives, either, but Connolly was checking.

"We want Rawley just as soon as we can get our hands on him," Roger said softly. He made a note to step up pressure in the search for Rawley, and then lit another cigarette, pondering.

Would it have made much difference if he had known before that Rawley was a chemist, with knowledge of and access to dangerous drugs?

His telephone bell rang, and he lifted the receiver promptly.

"West speaking."

"Hallo, Handsome, Dick Reed here," said the Superintendent on duty, with a quiet voice, "come along for a word, will you? I've got some odds and ends."

Reed was near retirement, a grey-haired, quiet-mannered man of nearly sixty, who looked as if he rightly belonged to the laboratory or the scholar's desk, but who had spent his life in the hurly-burly of the Yard.

He looked up from a big desk as Roger entered his room. "Hello," he greeted, "come and sit down." He waited. "You look as if you could do with some shut-eye."

"No mood for sleep, there's too much on my mind."

"We'd better have a noggin, then," said Reed, and bent down for a bottle of whisky and a soda syphon. "I hear they've been trying to axe you."

Roger grinned.

"When Waite's had time to cool off, I'll ask him what that axe was doing in his kitchen."

"I can tell you," said Reed. "A Boy Scout pal of his turned up here, and we asked him a few questions. Every now and again Waite goes tree felling in Surrey, a kind of keep-fit stunt with his other Boy Scouts."

"I'm not a bit sure that I'd like my boys to be in his troop," Roger mused, "but he can wait. I've other problems. Dick, know anything about the effects of heroin?"

"Plenty."

"And 'cures'?"

"A little."

"Ever known an addict, when having a cure, who wouldn't sell his soul in the early days for a shot in the arm?"

Reed said thoughtfully, "No. What's on your mind?"

"Mrs. Cunliffe's an addict. She's been in the Palli Clinic two or three times for these so-called cures. According to her husband, even the Clinic's staff hasn't been able to make her say where she gets the drugs."

"Oh, no," Reed said softly. "So someone's lying."

"Someone's lying, and from now on Cunliffe ought to be watched – and it's important that we trace Arthur Rawley."

"They may pick him up in the morning," Reed said. "I'll detail a watch on Cunliffe, too." He picked up a telephone and gave instructions, then jotted down a note on a memo pad. "Thanks," said Roger, "is that axe-wielder conscious?"

"No."

"*Anyone* conscious?"

"Mrs. Kitt's off the danger list, so we should be able to tackle her in the morning," said Reed, equably. "Waite is kicking his heels downstairs, and letting off steam every ten minutes or so. The Akers girl is in another room – coldly aloof, one might say." Reed grinned, then sipped his whisky. "Here's good hunting." Then he rummaged among the papers on his desk. "Since you found that opium and heroin, I've had a quick check over the known and suspected distributing agents and the other drug mobs. No big ones active at the moment, as far as we know. We can get everyone busy on that angle in the morning – how much of the stuff d'you think there was?"

"A pound or so of heroin, half a pound of snow."

"Wholesale, eh? If Waite's been distributing through his Campaign Committee—"

"Or if his Campaign Committee has been taking him for a ride," Roger said dryly. "I wish I knew how the man who set fire to those records came to know that we might be after them. Only Waite and the Akers girl knew. If the house was watched, or someone in one of the other flats—" He broke off. "Guesswork. Forget it. Anything else doing?"

"No. Why don't you go upstairs and have a rest? Kick your shoes off and put your head down."

"I want to see Jackson when he's back from Oxford," Roger said, but before Reed could comment, a telephone bell rang.

"Half a mo'," Reed said, and lifted the receiver. "Reed speaking … Yes, he's with me right now, who is it? … Oh, yes, put him through." He handed Roger the telephone as he spoke, and went on in the same quiet voice, "Mountain's come to you. It's Charles Jackson."

"Thanks," Roger said, and took the instrument hurriedly. "Hallo—"

"Is that *West*?" Jackson demanded, so loudly that the sound hurt Roger's ear.

It wasn't like Jackson to shout. He had fought against trying to interfere from the beginning. He felt like hell because his lovely young wife had disappeared, yet had kept his head – well enough to go to see Rosemary's mother, for instance. Now, he sounded as if he was ready to blow right up.

"West here," Roger said.

"West—" Jackson almost choked, and now Roger was alarmed. "Will you—come over at once? I—God, it's dreadful."

Dreadful?

It could be news of his Rosemary; it could be news that she was dead.

"What?" Roger began sharply.

"I'm at the flat," Jackson said, and put down the receiver; it clattered as if he hardly knew what he was doing.

Roger pushed his chair back and grabbed his hat from a corner of Reed's desk.

"Trouble, Jackson's place," he said, "we've a couple of men there, but may need more." He moved towards the door, as alert as if this was his first job of the day. "I'll call you."

He had never driven faster than he did to Haycourt Mews.

The light was blazing out from the bedroom window. A plainclothes C.I.D. man on duty at the corner of the mews stared at Roger as he jammed on the brakes and then jumped out of the car, and he came hurrying, perhaps a little edgy, not quite knowing what to expect. He recognised Roger as Roger said abruptly: "Hallo, Kimber. Anything to report?"

"Mr. Jackson got back about half an hour ago, sir."

"Anyone with him?"

"No, sir."

"Right, thanks," said Roger, and went up the stairs two at a time. The door opened, so he didn't need to ring. When he saw Jackson's face he knew that there must be real cause for despair; no man of his type would break down like this except under great pressure.

"All right," Roger said quietly. "What is it?"

It would not have surprised him had Jackson said that his wife was dead.

Jackson said, "Come and see for yourself."

He strode into the big living-room, with its pastel colours, and the *décor* which was so much at one with the grace and charm and prettiness of Rosemary Jackson. On a table, face upwards, were two photographs; near them was a large envelope, ripped open.

"Go on," Jackson rasped. "See for yourself."

Roger went forward.

He did not recognise the women in the pictures, although at first he had thought that they would be of Jackson's wife. One was young and nice looking, hardly beautiful but with a gaiety one couldn't mistake, and lips which looked as if they would laugh easily. The other was of a much older woman.

Older?

"Look on the back," Jackson said.

Roger turned them over.

He was beginning to understand already, for he could see the likeness in the two photographs; the shape of the forehead, the bone formation of cheek and nose were very much alike.

He read on the photograph of the young, happy woman, one word: *Before.*

He read on the photograph of the "older" woman, one word: *After.*

Then he noticed something which he hadn't seen before, because it was half covered by the ripped envelope; a newspaper cutting. He picked it up as Jackson began to talk in a hoarse, helpless voice.

"What are you going to do, West? How are you going to find her? You can't let it happen to her, West, do you hear? You can't let it happen, it's too awful even to think about." Roger was reading the opening paragraphs of the recent Home Office report on the activity of dope rings in Great Britain – a cold, detached analysis, a model of its kind and drawn up by Jackson, as secretary to the Committee of Inquiry.

What did it add up to?

"What are you going to do to find her?" Jackson asked roughly. "You've got to find her!"

Roger said quietly, "What are you going to do?"

"There isn't a thing I can!"

Roger eyed him levelly.

"Sure about that?"

"What the devil are you driving at?"

"I think I'll give it to you straight," Roger said. "There are two factors in this case – dope is one, and you've just drawn up that report, it's your own home ground. The witnesses and others concerned in the case against Cunliffe, four years ago, following the death of Mrs. Rawley. I don't pretend to know how they tie up, but I do know that two witnesses in that case have been murdered, that you and Mrs. Kitt have run into trouble, that Waite, who was behind the prosecution, was nearly killed tonight."

Jackson said roughly, "What's that to do with my wife's disappearance?"

"Two people have been murdered, two nearly murdered, you've been attacked," Roger said. "There could be one reason for all the crimes – to keep everyone concerned from talking. Have they kidnapped your wife to make sure you don't talk?"

"What the hell should I have to talk about?"

"I'm asking you," Roger said. "We've got every policeman in the county looking for your wife, but if we can't save her because of information you're withholding, you can't blame us."

"I'm not holding back a thing," Jackson growled.

Roger drove straight back to the Yard, saw Reed again, and with Reed's help put everything in hand for the next morning's efforts.

There was a new angle now, and one he had to try: was Jackson taking any kind of chance with his wife? The man was undoubtedly in torment, and might be under almost unbearable pressure.

"We need to check his work on that Commission, find out the people he interviewed, and see if we can find an association with this job," Roger said briskly.

"Right," Reed agreed.

Every man on the list which Roger had made out at Waite's apartment would be rounded up and brought in for questioning, and a general call was out for news of Arthur Rawley.

Waite hadn't yet talked, and he was sleeping; they would give him a little while longer, and then start questioning him about everyone who had access to the Campaign Headquarters.

All people remotely connected with the defence of the old case against Cunliffe were given double protection. Roger plugged every loophole he could find. Directly the doctors agreed, Mrs. Kitt would be questioned, and Dr. Kitt would be questioned again exhaustively; if the police could find out why Mrs. Kitt had been blackmailed, and who was blackmailing her, it might crack open the case.

Chatworth would have approved of everything; and Chatworth would have shared Roger's and the Yard's fears for Rosemary Jackson.

The news about the Assistant Commissioner had not changed.

Roger went upstairs to a dormitory of beds and bunks. It was four o'clock before he put his head down, and he was asleep within minutes. He slept heavily, but woke without being called; it was nearly half-past six.

Razors and everything he needed were available.

He had a shave and a cold shower, then went downstairs, but it was too early to begin to check results, and nothing new had come in. He went to the canteen for some tea, drank it piping hot, and went to his own office. It was full daylight, and the cleaners were in. He checked that nothing important was on his desk, then went downstairs to the waiting-rooms, to see Waite and June Akers. A duty sergeant said that Waite had dozed on and off during the night, in an easy-chair. The girl seemed to have slept for several hours; a policewoman was with her now, while she was washing.

"All right to go in, sir," the policeman said, a few minutes later.

Roger went in.

It was not hard to believe that the girl had slept well for some time. She looked fresh and rested, and obviously her headache had gone. Her eyes were her loveliest feature, very clear and quite beautiful. Take away their beauty and the smoothness of her complexion, and she would be a tall girl with a nice figure and a round face.

"Good morning," Roger said. "Sit down, please."

"I would rather stand." She was calm but aloof.

"Please yourself." Roger looked at her coldly, and he didn't have to pretend. Undoubtedly she had known that heroin was in that cabinet. "I want some information from you which might save several lives, and which might save a lot of people from wrecking their lives. And I'm not fooling." He pulled out the photographs which Jackson had given him. "Ever seen anything like this?"

June looked down at the photographs and the captions, *Before* and *After*, now stuck on to the front. She flinched, shot a glance at Roger, and then said:

"Yes, I have. In magazines."

"That stuff which was found at the Campaign office does this kind of thing to women," he said roughly. "These photographs were sent to the husband of a woman who was kidnapped yesterday. It looks as if she's going to be driven mad in the same way. That's just one of the reasons why we're going to find out who's handling that drug, and how they got into that cabinet."

She stood still and silent.

He flashed at her: "Why was your aunt being blackmailed? She was paying more money to blackmailers than she could afford. Let's have it—why?"

There was a short, tense pause. The girl's defiance was weakened by obvious anxiety, she was not so sure of herself. So Mrs. Kitt was her weak spot.

"Your aunt was buying drugs, is that it?" Roger rasped. "She was paying out ten pounds every month which she couldn't afford because she had to have drugs to satisfy her craving." When June didn't answer, he went on roughly, "I can get the medical report and check on this within an hour or so, you're only wasting time. Is that what was happening?"

After a pause, the girl said, "No, it wasn't, she—she was being blackmailed."

"Why?"

"I—I don't have to answer."

"That's right," Roger said, "you don't have to answer. You can withhold vital evidence, you can endanger the lives of other people, you can think yourself a heroine – but you don't have to answer and there's no way I can make you. But there's a way I can put you and Waite in dock, there's a way—"

"She—she was being blackmailed because my uncle once sold narcotics illegally," June said very quietly. "It happened years ago, and he only did it once. If it were known, it would ruin him and break her heart."

"Has she been supplying the blackmailer with drugs from her husband's surgery?"

"She—"

"*Has she?*"

"I don't know," June said in a low-pitched voice.

## Chapter Nineteen

# False Reports

This was the moment to ease off the pressure, when the velvet glove might get better results. Roger watched the girl for what must have seemed a long time. Agitation showed in her eyes, yet he thought that she felt a measure of relief; certainly she no longer had difficulty in meeting his gaze.

"When did she tell you this?" Roger asked, in a much milder tone.

"Six months or more ago."

"Was Peter Waite the blackmailer?"

"I don't believe that Peter knows anything about it," June said steadily. "I think Peter's been used by the men who are distributing drugs. I suppose—I suppose I'd better tell you everything from the beginning. When I found out that my aunt was being blackmailed, it worried me a great deal."

Roger interrupted. "You're pretty close to her, are you?"

"Aunt Liz? Yes, she's been—well, that doesn't matter. We've been more like mother and daughter. She brought me up."

"When did you begin to suspect that she was in trouble?"

"Three years or so ago, I suppose," said June, and went to a chair and sat down. "First I realised that she wasn't well. She had nervous spasms, sometimes she would break down and cry over the simplest things, at other times she seemed more vigorous and strong than ever. I thought she was working too hard – she never seems to stop doing something," June went on, "she's at this committee or that, she's on the Bench, she's the most energetic woman in the world – and these bad patches didn't come very often at first. Then I began to notice that if I saw her on a Monday evening or a Tuesday morning, she was very edgy. When I asked her about it, she snapped and called it nonsense. I began to call on Tuesdays, and one day a man came to see her. I heard her shouting at him. He was a nasty little man with a snub nose, and when he left he was grinning. He—"

"Did he come by car?"

"Yes."

"Did you notice what car?"

"Yes," said June, "it was an Iso. I'd seen it outside once or twice when I'd come on Tuesdays. That day I made her tell me, and I think she was glad to confide in someone."

"How long had it been going on, do you know?"

"No, she wouldn't talk much about it, she was so desperately anxious not to let Uncle know."

"Did you tell him?"

"Of course not."

"What did you do?"

"I suppose it was silly," she said, "but I tried to find out who was behind it, and the next Tuesday I followed the man when he called. He—"

"Did your aunt know his name?"

"She knew him as Brown," June said. "That's the only name I ever heard."

"Go on, please," Roger said, "Where did he go?"

"To Peter's Campaign Headquarters," June said. She sat clasping her hands in front of her, and her eyes were very bright, as with fear. "When I realised that it was this Parson Pete, I—well, I wanted to come to the police right away. Of course I should have done. But it might have meant betraying my aunt and uncle, and after her lifetime of public service that would have been cruelly humiliating; I really believe that it would have killed them. I pretended to want to help in the Accident Prevention Campaign, and thought I might be able to save Aunt Liz from being blackmailed."

She stopped again, but this wasn't the moment to remind her that loyalty to her aunt had blinded her to simple duty. "Yes," Roger said.

"The most unexpected thing happened," June told him, very quietly.

"Yes?"

"I began to respect Peter Waite. When I first met him, I hated the very sight of him, but soon I began to doubt whether he knew anything about any crimes. He seemed so transparently honest, and although nearly everyone thinks he's crazy about road accidents, I began to believe that *he* was sane and the rest of us crazy." Her gaze was very direct. "When you study his arguments closely, they do make sense. All he asks is that the penalties for careless driving be made a hundred times greater than they are, so that people dare not be careless, and that all the laws against motorists be enforced."

"So you fell in love with him," Roger remarked dryly. "How long ago was this?"

"Only a few months," said June. "At first I just didn't know what to make of the situation. Then I discovered that a lot of people had access to the Campaign Rooms. At least half a dozen committee members had keys, and probably others could get in and out of the flat whether Peter was there or not. I didn't want to tell Peter until I was fairly sure what was happening, and so I began to try to find out who did come when he wasn't there."

She clasped her hands so tightly that the knuckles went white.

"Then I saw that several of the campaign workers looked peculiar, and I realised that they took drugs. So did people who called to make inquiries – often the same people, week after week. It wasn't until the past few days that I realised that it was a drug-distributing centre. I just didn't know what to do. I was afraid that if Peter was told he would collapse, and—and anyhow, how could I be sure that the police would think that he was innocent? Even *I* wasn't sure."

Roger could tell her that she had been crazy, but he could understand what had gone on in her mind. She had kept her knowledge to herself out of that sense of loyalty, not out of fear.

"How many of these men actually handled the drugs? Do you know?"

"You took their names and addresses last night," June said.

"Did you tell anyone else that I'd taken those names and addresses?"

"No."

"Did Waite tell anyone?"

"He couldn't have done. I was with him all the time – you ought to know that."

"*Every* minute?"

"Yes, every minute," June insisted. "He couldn't have warned anyone that you were interested in the committee, but—well, I know that his flat was watched last night. I saw the man Brown, he had been there several times, just watching."

"Did you ever see a Mr. or a Mrs. Jackson there?"

"No – Peter went to see a Mrs. Jackson, because her husband was on some Government Committee; he tried every possible kind of contact. But it turned out that her husband was an old acquaintance who wasn't likely to help."

"Sure Jackson didn't visit the Campaign Rooms?"

"He didn't while I was there."

"How about a Mrs. Cunliffe?"

"Yes, there was a Mrs. Cunliffe, a few weeks ago," June said, "a very smart woman, who didn't come again."

Roger asked more questions, but learned nothing more, and finally he said: "All right, Miss Akers, thank you. I'll want all this in the form of a statement, you can dictate it to a shorthand-writer, or write it down yourself. Now I'll go and see Peter Waite." He moved to the door, but turned to look at her. "Make sure everything you say is absolutely true, remember we shall check every word in every way we can."

"I've told you the whole truth," she said simply.

Roger was inclined to believe that she had.

When he questioned Waite, he found the man rested and in a much calmer mood. It was difficult to believe that he had organised anything except his campaign, his life's work. He agreed that Mrs. Cunliffe had been a contributor and helper, that he had a committee member named Brown, that after visiting Mrs. Jackson he had realised who her husband was. "Had you met him since the Ligate case?"

"I knew him quite well in Ligate," Waite said. "When I realised that it was the same Jackson, I didn't waste any more time."

"Did you know Sergeant Atkinson?"

"Very slightly."

"A Mrs. Bray?"

"Oh, yes," said Waite, "Mrs. Bray helped me for years, but she had to stop, unfortunately. I haven't seen her for nearly a year."

"She was run down and killed by a car," Roger said abruptly. "Didn't you know?"

"Mrs. *Bray*," breathed Waite, and the light of his fervour came back to his eyes. "After all she'd done – it's diabolical! Why, she—"

"Mr. Waite, can you explain the presence in your Campaign room of a substantial quantity of narcotics – of dangerous drugs?"

Waite looked completely bewildered, even incredulous.

If that was an act, it was a brilliant one.

Roger left Waite making a statement to a shorthand-writer and went back to his office. Reports were coming in fast, but most of them were negative. There was nothing new about Jackson, but a man watching the mews telephoned to say that Jackson was up.

Roger went to see him. He looked haggard and distraught, but still maintained that he was hiding nothing.

"All right," Roger said, "let's approach it from another angle. Someone's been getting at you, trying to wreck your marriage, finally kidnapping your wife. Either she's been under pressure but hasn't told you, or else you've some dangerous knowledge you don't know about. We now know that narcotics are behind this business. Work at that, will you? Go over that report, check everything you learned – try to recall anything that you know and which might be dangerous."

"Dangerous to whom?" Jackson demanded.

"Anyone," Roger said. "Possibly you learned something without knowing how significant it was."

Before going to the Yard, Roger drove to Ligate, and took Connolly with him to see Dr. Kitt. The old man was frail and seemed untroubled, but when challenged with the years-old crime, he broke down completely.

He swore that he had not known that his wife had been blackmailed.

When Roger reached the Yard, reports were in of several of Waite's Campaign Committee men. One after another was detained by two C.I.D. men for questioning, all protesting. Their homes and their clothes were searched, and in the case of six members of the committee, traces of heroin were found in the linings of pockets, or in drawers and cupboards.

The pressure on these six men could be stepped up, but it was impossible to be sure that they knew who was behind it. So far, all had denied knowing a thing, and it might be hours before any of them began to crack.

And Rosemary Jackson was still missing.

Arthur Rawley was not traced.

A report from Ligate said that Atkinson's wife had won a big dividend on Ansett's pools, so on the surface of this, that story was genuine. It had to be checked. Ansett's Head Office was in London, and Roger went there himself. A puzzled director said no, the records of all winners were never destroyed, and if the police wanted to search, they were most welcome.

The search did not take long.

No one named Atkinson was among the big dividend winners, and no one from a Ligate address.

So Mrs. Atkinson hadn't won a fortune on the pools.

Roger went to see her straight away. She was tearful when he arrived, and it was difficult to broach the subject, with the pretty daughter looking on, resenting the questions.

Mrs. Atkinson swore that she didn't know where her husband had got the money, he'd told her it was on the pools.

Neither Rosemary Jackson nor Rawley was found that day.

But three members of the Campaign Committee talked, each statement being identical with the others. They received their supplies of opium and heroin at the Campaign Headquarters, and Brown handed it out. There had been a false drawer in a filing-cabinet where he kept some of the stuff. Each had a list of customers, on whom they called regularly with supplies, and they wrote down as many of the customers' names and addresses as they could from memory.

Waite himself had never given any drugs to them.

All of them had jobs which took them into private homes – two were radio and television technicians, one an insurance agent, two were door-to-door salesmen, one was a baker. They kept ten per cent of the money they collected and put the rest into the false drawer, when Brown wasn't there to collect it.

And as Roger, Cortland and members of the Yard's vice squad studied the statements, one question became more and more insistent.

"Could all this have happened at Waite's Campaign Headquarters without Waite knowing?" Cortland asked rather impatiently. "You're about the only one who thinks it's possible, Handsome."

"And I could be wrong," Roger said mildly, "but before we have all the answers, we want to know where Mrs. Atkinson and Mrs. Bray got that money. We also want to know where Rawley is – whether he is dead or alive. We want to know why the doctors treating Mrs. Cunliffe at the Palli Clinic can't get a simple answer from her. We want—"

"Okay, okay," said Cortland, "you've made your point."

"What about this man Brown, is he talking yet?" Roger asked.

"Still unconscious – and *you* hit him."

"And I'd hit him again. How about Mrs. Kitt?"

"She had a relapse, but we'll get at her soon," said Cortland. "Meanwhile we keep at it."

That included the time-taking task of questioning Waite's neighbours, the people in the other flats, tradesmen and postmen and everyone familiar with the district, to try to compile a longer list of the regular visitors to the Campaign Headquarters. Waite gave them over a hundred names, and everyone was visited.

Hour in, hour out, the police checked and rejected reports that Rosemary Jackson had been found; they looked for Arthur Rawley, and kept at the Campaign helpers. Every Division concentrated most of its plain-clothes and some of the uniformed men on to the task. A hundred Pyes and a hundred Davises were on the go all day, yet nothing more was found.

Cunliffe's movements were quite unsuspicious, and he visited the Palli Clinic in the afternoon, to see his wife.

Jackson said that he could think of nothing that might help.

The Yard was checking the resident and consulting staff at the Clinic, particularly a Dr. Smith, who was in charge of Mrs. Cunliffe's cures; they didn't yet understand why he hadn't managed to make her tell where she obtained her supplies.

Early the next morning, there were two developments.

Brown recovered consciousness, and Mrs. Kitt was able to talk.

Brown's head was a mass of bandages, his eyes looked sunken, his lips twitched. He was suffering from lack of heroin, and the doctors had decided to give him a shot. He talked in a hoarse voice, just such a voice as that of the man who had telephoned Rosemary Jackson.

He said that he had attacked West simply to escape, and that he took his orders from and paid the money over to Peter Waite.

Cortland and other Yard men almost chortled.

Straight from Brown, Roger went to see Mrs. Kitt.

Driving him with a sense of desperation was not only Waite and June Akers, but the need to find Rosemary Jackson.

Was she alive?

Was she drugged?

Was she at the beginning of a life of horror?

## Chapter Twenty

## Dream World

In the periods during which she was fully conscious and without the stimulus of the drug, Rosemary knew that it could be the beginning of the life of horror. Two or three times a day, she felt her nerves getting raw and her patience breaking, while she sat alone in the small room. The bed was in one corner and the blank window and the door were closed and locked. She tried to look into the future, which she could not really see.

She could picture Charles and imagine how he was feeling; she felt a sense of utter hopelessness and despair, and yet—

She looked forward to the moment when the door would open and a man would come in carrying a hypodermic needle.

She would look forward to the moment of sharp pain as the needle went in, would see the tiny globule of blood, and watch it, smiling tautly, at once fearful and yet eager. She knew it would change her mood, that soon afterwards she would forget the horrors, the edginess, the desire to shout and scream and rage. She would begin to live in that dream world, and realised vaguely that it would not be long before the dream world, to her, was true reality; and the other – the world without her drug – the nightmare.

In her dreams, she did not think of Charles.

## Chapter Twenty-One

# Statement from Mrs. Kitt

The small ward in the Ligate Hospital where Mrs. Kitt lay was bright with pale-green shiny paint, and brighter with a mass of flowers, some on the window-sill, some on a table, some on a trolley at the foot of her bed. Daffodils and tulips, narcissi and violets, roses and carnations – each with a little card attached, wishing her well. They came from the other members of the magisterial bench, from the police, from the Borough Council, from committees on which she served, from private well-wishers.

She was sitting up a little on her pillow when Roger arrived, an old woman with very bright eyes and sunken cheeks, with a jaw which jutted out more because her cheeks had dropped so much, with a great hooked nose – a kind of skeleton of the terror of the Bench that she had been. Yet there was nothing of death in her eyes, and there was vigour in her voice and in her manner.

"So you're this glamorous policeman," she said. Her voice was weak, but that seemed to make little difference to her spirit. "Lucky you kept out of my court, I'd glamorise you! What is it you want to know? I've been trying to protect my husband from a lunatic mistake he made, ten years or more ago. And I'd do it again."

No doubt she would, if she had the chance.

"Who collected the blackmail money?" Roger asked.

"A man calling himself Brown."

"Always the same man?"

"Yes."

"How much did you pay him?"

"Ten pounds each visit."

"Is that all?"

"It was more than I could afford."

"Did you also pay in kind, Mrs. Kitt?"

"If you mean, did I give him heroin or any other drugs from the surgery, no, I did not."

It was hard not to believe that.

"Did you ever refuse to pay?"

"I tried to."

"What happened?"

"I couldn't go through with it."

"Did you know anyone else who was blackmailing you besides Brown?"

"No."

"Have you any idea how anyone discovered that Dr. Kitt had once supplied narcotics illegally?"

The sharp features seemed to become sharper, the eyes brighter.

"Yes." declared Mrs. Kitt.

"How?"

"It was done through a chemist who was in Ligate at the time – a man named Rawley. Either he told a third party at the time, or later."

"How long did you know that Rawley dealt in drugs, illegally?"

"I didn't know until the blackmail began, and he'd left Ligate by then," said Mrs. Kitt.

In spite of her vigour, she was feeling the strain, and it wouldn't be long before the doctor stopped the questioning. So Roger asked quietly, "Have you any idea why you were attacked the other night, Mrs. Kitt?"

"Yes," she said, and this time she closed her eyes. "Yes, I have. Last week I told Brown I couldn't go on, that he was ruining me, that I'd have to tell the police if he didn't stop. So I suppose I frightened him."

Probably she had, thought Roger; probably that explained the attack on her, but it left everything else unexplained. "Now, please," the doctor began.

"Just one more question," Roger said. "Have you any reason to believe that the Rev. Peter Waite is involved, Mrs. Kitt?"

She smiled. "Peter Waite," she echoed, and her voice grew stronger. "No, I have not. That man's a saint." She didn't wait for Roger to comment, but rushed on: "I've always fought against the victimisation of the motorist, and please God I always will, but I've wondered how much there was to be said on the other side, and I admire *guts*, sir, *guts*. It takes courage to keep working as young Peter Waite kept working. Everyone deserted him, yet he kept on – even after the Rawley case, when any ordinary human being would have known he hadn't a chance, he kept going. He used to write to me, protesting against every outrageous statement I made from the Bench—oh, I know I talk too much! After a while I decided I'd like to see this prophet. He isn't good looking, he hasn't much of a presence, he's got no money, he tries to take care of a flock of so-called sheep in a church which is bankrupt of money and ideas – I wanted to find out what drove him on, why he wouldn't let up. So I went to see him."

Roger said quietly, "That was some moment for Parson Pete?"

She gave a grin which, if she'd had more strength, would have had a touch of ferocity.

"You couldn't be more right, it was a red-letter day for Parson Pete! I can see him now, gaping at me when he opened the front door of that rabbit hutch he lives in. I went right in. I saw what he was trying to do, too, I knew that hardly another man in the world would have gone on trying, after the failures he'd had. That wasn't the only time I went to see him. I went five or six times, and I *thought* I understood what drove him. *Faith,* sir. That young man had simple faith – absolute conviction that he was right, absolute conviction that if we did what he wanted, punished everyone with terrible severity for carelessness on the roads, we would stop accidents. There he was, standing at that silly little desk in that big barn of a room with a lot of kindergarten daubs on the wall, pointing at the newspaper headlines one Christmas-time. In the same issue of the same paper, there were two reports. *Record Road Deaths over Christmas, nearly 200 Die, 7,000 Injured,* said one, and the other, *Brewers and Distillers Anticipate Record Sales this Christmas.* Yes, I can see them now," went on Mrs. Kitt, and she raised a weakly clenched hand. " 'So you're going to deny us a little Christmas cheer now,' I said to him, and he gave me such a reproachful look, he has eyes like a dog I sometimes think, and he said, 'You don't understand any more than the rest, Mrs. Kitt. I don't want to deny anyone anything, I want to help them to live longer to enjoy life. I'm not against liquor, I'm against any man or woman drinking just before driving a motor car. It isn't the only factor that makes a motor car lethal, but it's one of them. What I can't understand,' he went on – and he began to get worked up then, that's his trouble, he gets worked up too quickly – 'what I can't understand, Mrs. Kitt, is why you don't admit that the scientifically proved figures are right, that if you have alcohol in your blood before driving, your reactions aren't so good. You may not mean to, but you can easily become a killer.

" 'That's all I want to do,' he went on, 'I want to stop people from being killers and maimers of their fellow human beings. I've come to the conclusion that the only thing that will stop them killing others on the road is *fear.* Mrs. Kitt, put the fear of God into them with severe penalties, frightening penalties; *then* they'll see sense.'"

Mrs. Kitt stopped.

Her eyes glittered, too, and the doctor who had been in the room with them glanced at West and made it clear that there must be little more of this. The injured woman was breathing very hard, there was sweat on her forehead and a little beading on her upper lip.

Then, she said in a clear voice, "That was why I told Brown I couldn't go on. I couldn't get Waite's absolute integrity out of my mind. I began to hate myself for all I'd done. I felt I had to start afresh. Brown wouldn't believe that I meant it, so I told him that I had written a letter to the police – if he threatened me again, I would post it."

"When did you tell him that?" Roger asked quickly.

"On the morning I was attacked," she said. "I suppose the letter was gone."

"Yes," said Roger, "he took it all right. Did you hide it among your newspaper cuttings?"

"Yes," answered Mrs. Kitt.

That sounded like the truth. Whether it was or not, the doctor put up a commanding hand, as Mrs. Kitt fell back on to her pillows and closed her eyes.

Roger, Connolly and the shorthand-writer who had been taking everything down, went outside. The shorthand-writer hurried off to transcribe his notes, and Connolly said: "She'll stick to that, Handsome, and I should say we know why she was attacked and why there was such a mess."

"Yes," Roger agreed, "and the man tried to burn everything that might have pointed to blackmail."

"But it doesn't let Waite out," Cortland said.

"No, it doesn't," Roger said thoughtfully. "I'll go and talk to him again."

Back at the Yard, he checked reports, found nothing to help, and went next to see June Akers, who had signed her statement and was free to go. She had waited so as to see Roger, and outside the room where Waite was being held, she asked: "Have you charged him with anything yet?"

There was courage and defiance, and there was also fear in her. She was the second member of her family to become absolutely pro-Waite when she had got to know him, and Roger believed that it would take great quality to win such affection.

Could Waite have fooled them?

Remember, Brown had named him. Remember, too, that another of Brown's confreres had nearly killed him.

"Have you?" the girl insisted.

"No," Roger answered.

"Has he seen a solicitor?"

"No."

"I'll make sure that he soon does," June said, and Roger felt even more admiration for her. He couldn't hold Waite much longer without making a charge, anyhow, and once the charge was made, he would have to offer the man legal aid. But he waited for an hour after June had gone, until a telephone call came from a firm of Ligate solicitors who said that they were acting on Waite's behalf.

"Come and see him by all means," Roger said, and went straight downstairs. Waite looked up, showing momentary eagerness, which faded when he saw Roger's expression – and saw the sergeant who had come with Roger.

Now was the time for shock tactics.

"Peter Dylan Waite," Roger said abruptly, "it is my duty to arrest you on a charge of having in your possession a quantity of dangerous habit-forming drugs, commonly known as opium and heroin, and of distributing quantities of the said drugs to your friends and associates for profit. I must warn you that anything you say may be taken down and used as evidence."

Waite said almost proudly, "That is nonsense. I am not guilty."

By then, it was lunch-time.

By then, hundreds of reports, both of Rosemary Jackson and Arthur Rawley, had come in, and more hundreds had already been discredited. Jackson had telephoned three times, and Roger called him back immediately; but Jackson had nothing to report, only the desperate question to ask: "Have you found my wife?"

"The moment we have any news, we'll tell you," Roger promised.

"For God's sake find her!" Jackson shouted. "Why don't you find her?"

It wasn't easy to answer him.

Roger finished the call at last, went to Cortland's office. The Superintendent was alone, obviously snowed under with work, as obviously not quite capable of keeping smooth control as easily as Chatworth.

"Hallo, Handsome. I was just going to ask you how things are moving."

"They've almost stopped."

"Hell of a job, isn't it? Well, just had one bit of more cheerful news," Cortland went on. "Latest word from the hospital is that Chatworth is a bit better. Too early to say anything definite yet, but I gather that he really has a chance now. I'm told that after a packet like this he won't ever be good for a big job again, but even if he gets well enough to enjoy himself for a bit, it would be something."

For the first time for days, Roger felt as if he could be light-hearted without too much effort. It didn't last long.

"Now, the big job," said Cortland. "Until we find Mrs. Jackson, we're going to be screwed up to maximum effort. I don't mind telling you that we're taking men off other jobs which are pretty urgent, too. The tie-up with the murder of Atkinson makes it worse. Now we know it's connected with dope, there's going to be one long shriek for results. The first bit of prodding is in the *Daily Globe*. Seen it?"

"They're shaken because Waite's place was fired when the house was supposed to have been watched," Roger said, "and they've got a case."

"Yes. Like to know what I think, Handsome?"

"It's what I'm here for."

"Even if Waite isn't mixed up in it, he can put a finger on everyone who is. At the moment, he's on his dignity, but when he gets over that and realises what will probably happen to him, he'll put his thinking cap on. Whoever is behind it is in acute danger from Waite. Stands to reason – they tried to kill him, didn't they?"

Roger didn't speak.

"If we let Waite out on bail, or even release him before he goes up before the beak, we might provoke an attack on him," Cortland went on, "and if he's watched like a lynx, we'll catch whoever tries to attack without allowing him to be hurt. I know it's risky, but— well, what do you think of it?"

"I hate the idea," Roger said bluntly, "but we might have to come to it. I'm going to have a stab at getting a statement from Mrs. Cunliffe. I'm told she's at the tail end of a cure, and able to talk sense. Okay?"

"Try anything," Cortland said.

That was almost a cry of desperation, and there was a lot of reason in it, too. As *locum tenens* to Chatworth, Cortland felt the crushing weight of responsibility, and needed quick results. Jackson had undoubtedly been pushing hard through his friends, too – as a partner in a law firm with considerable influence. If men like Old Nod – Sir Wilfred Treaze, Q.C. – could harass Chatworth, how much more could they harass Cortland? Oh, it was easy to understand Cortland's desperation, Jackson's dread, the newspaper pressure and the impatience of the whole of the police force to get results.

Roger had left Cortland's office, and was actually on the way to his car, when a sergeant came running down the steps after him.

"Mr. West, sir!"

"Hallo?" Roger turned round.

"Mr. Jackson's on the telephone, sir, and he says that he must speak to you, it's desperately urgent. I just happened—"

Roger raced back to the hall and grabbed the telephone off the duty sergeant's desk.

"West here," he said, "put Mr. Jackson through to me."

"Yes, sir."

There was only a moment's delay before Roger heard Jackson, with a new note of urgency in his voice. Here was news of a kind; of disaster or of hope.

"West, I think I've got it."

"Got what?"

"The answer you're looking for, the Palli Clinic—"

"What about it?" Roger felt his heart hammering.

"That's where the powder and lipstick were put in my clothes. I was there several times during the Committee inquiry, and saw several of the patients, while members of the Committee were getting voluntary statements. There was a woman who flung her arms round me, I had a hell of a job to get away from her. West, I'm positive, and I'm going there to—"

"You keep away from the Clinic," Roger said swiftly. "This is our job. Is there anything else?"

"I'm not—I'm not positive, but I've been going over everything I was told at the Clinic, taking my mind back to every interview I had, and there was one man whom I didn't see until the last minute, he kept sending someone else. He—"

"*Who?*"

"The Resident Medical Officer, a Dr. Smith. There was something familiar about him, I've only just realised what it was. He—he's Rawley. You know, Rawley, the husband of the woman whom Cunliffe knocked down, who—"

"That's all I need," Roger said softly. "Jackson, I know it's hell, but stay where you are until we send word. Don't do a thing which might warn Rawley."

"If I haven't heard from you within an hour, I'm going to the Clinic myself," Jackson growled.

"Just what have we got?" Cortland asked, and he couldn't keep the excitement out of his voice.

"Plenty," said Roger. "We know that Rawley dealt in snow years ago. He's now a so-called doctor at a private clinic specialising in drug-addiction cures. He tried to dodge Jackson, because he feared he would be recognised as Rawley. Cunliffe's wife is at the Clinic, where they say they can't make her admit where she gets her dope from, but that was always unbelievable. Rawley's the likely blackmailer of Mrs. Kitt, too. If Rawley is the kingpin, a lot hangs together. If that's not enough—"

"It is. What've you done?" demanded Cortland.

"Had a cordon put round the Clinic, so that no one from there can get away if we want 'em stopped," Roger said, "but it's pretty far out, we don't want our chaps seen. I've a Squad laundry van near the main gates to radio to the cordon, and a Squad taxi at the back."

"Right. What then?"

"The man I'm not at all sure about is Cunliffe," Roger said, "so I'm going to phone and ask his permission to go and visit his wife. If anyone starts moving from the Clinic in a hurry, we can be pretty sure he's warned them."

"But Handsome—his own wife—"

"Rawley's wife died, didn't she?" Roger said grimly. "Perhaps we'll soon know why."

"By all means talk to my wife," Cunliffe said to Roger on the telephone, "and if anyone at the Clinic wants my personal authority, ask them to speak to me on the telephone, will you?"

"Thanks very much," Roger said.

"I suppose everything *is* worth trying," Cunliffe said, "but I confess I'm not very optimistic. I've tried so often to find out more from her."

"I'll let you know if anything comes of it," Roger promised, and rang off.

The Palli Clinic was a large house near Hampstead Heath, with a tall brick wall running all round it. It looked pleasant enough, and the grounds were well kept. Two large cars stood in the long driveway, and the only thing which seemed even remotely sinister were the bars at several of the windows, and the fact that most of the barred windows were glazed with frosted glass, so that the inmates couldn't see out, and people outside couldn't see in.

Roger gave his name and card to a middle-aged receptionist, and was kept waiting only for five minutes. Then he was taken along a wide, carpeted passage to a room where a small, plump, shiny-faced man with a lot of dark hair and a small dark beard sat behind a large, shiny and imposing-looking desk. Roger's first impression was of a phoney, but this was Reginald Gee, the secretary, who had been in that position for years.

He had an unexpectedly high-pitched voice.

"How can I help you, Chief Inspector? I'll be glad to do anything I can, of course, anything I can."

"Thank you," Roger said formally. "I'd like a talk with Mrs. Cunliffe. I want to try to find out how she gets access to the heroin."

"Talk to her by all means," said Gee. "Believe me, if you can find out where she's got it from and so stop her from getting it again, then both she and her husband will have cause to bless you! We've tried every way we know, and failed."

Only a man who was not familiar with addicts' desperation could believe that. Gee must be familiar, so he was lying.

Didn't he realise that Roger would know that?

"I'll gladly come with you myself," Gee said. "We want to give you as much help as we can."

He led the way up one flight of stairs, and then into a pleasantly furnished room which might have been in any good-class hotel. Sitting on a window-seat, and looking into the grounds, was Cunliffe's wife.

At the first glimpse of her, Roger felt sure she had been told he was coming. She looked at him tensely, a middle-aged woman with the greying hair and faded skin, and all the signs of a vanished beauty.

She pretended to show no great interest when Roger was introduced, yet was obviously on edge and frightened. But that hardly mattered, and he was at least as much on edge.

This was the woman of the two photographs which had been sent to Jackson – *Before* and *After*. "After" was a strikingly good likeness.

That wasn't all. He'd sent for samples of Angeli's *Nocturne,* and he recognised the smell. Mrs. Cunliffe used the perfume and powder which had been found in Charles Jackson's pockets – the powder put there to make his Rosemary suspect there was another woman.

Rosemary Jackson.

She was dozing, dreamily, in a room almost immediately above the one where Roger stood.

## Chapter Twenty-Two

# Deadly Question

Outside, the sun was shining, the lawns looked bright and the flower-beds were freshly dug, some daffodils were in full bloom. Outside, beyond the walls of the nursing home, was a tall sign – *Garage, Austin Service*. Outside were people moving about freely and traffic bustling – outside, too, was the Yard car which, had brought Roger here, and the sergeant would be sitting at the wheel, ostensibly reading a newspaper, actually keeping his eyes wide open. There was a grocery van instead of the laundry van, and a post-office vehicle in place of the taxi at the rear.

Inside the nursing home was frightened Mrs. Cunliffe, with Roger.

The fear showed in her eyes, in the way her lips worked, in the trembling of her hands. She couldn't keep them still, and stared at Roger as if she hated the sight of him.

"Good morning, Mrs. Cunliffe," said Gee in his rather high-pitched voice, "we have a visitor to see you – Chief Inspector West of New Scotland Yard. There is no need to be distressed, the Chief Inspector is only anxious to help you, like all of us – that's all we want to do. Isn't it, Chief Inspector?"

"I—I don't need any help," Vera Cunliffe said. "I'm better, I'm much better. You know I am, Mr. Gee! But I don't like meeting people, you know I don't like meeting them."

"That's just a little nervousness, you'll soon get over the freshness of meeting the Chief Inspector," said Gee, speaking as if he was talking to a child. "There's nothing at all to worry about, and he only wants to ask you one or two simple questions. Do try to answer."

"I—I've such a terrible headache, I can't think of anything, I just can't—can't think."

She was too frightened to think.

Her fear might spring from the drug addiction, or might have a more urgent cause. Her gaze flickered from Roger to Gee, and if Roger had to put money on it, he would say that she was much more frightened of the Clinic's secretary than she was of him.

"Of course you can think, Mrs. Cunliffe," Gee said in a chiding voice, "your mind is quite as clear as mine. You mustn't get so upset on meeting strangers; after all, you'll be going home very soon, and you don't want to be so nervous then, do you? It's perfectly all right for you to answer the Chief Inspector's questions, just tell him the simple truth – and I'm sure that he will do all he can to help you. We really don't want you to go through the tortures of a cure and then go away and start getting the drugs again, do we?"

She didn't answer, but watched Roger as if dreading what he was going to ask. One thing was certain: he must not ask anything which would drive her farther over the edge of terror. But he had to ask questions which would justify his visit.

"Do you remember the name of anyone who has given you the drug?" Roger asked.

"I—I don't remember. I've told everyone that I don't remember, I—"

"Have you ever met a Reverend Peter Waite, who runs a Road Safety Campaign?"

She darted a glance at Gee, as if to find out whether she was allowed to answer that.

"Do answer the Chief Inspector, Mrs. Cunliffe, please."

"I—yes, yes," she said anxiously. "I helped Mr. Waite."

"Did you ever go to his apartment at 188, Fields View?"

"Y—y—yes, I—I did some work for him there, my—my husband wanted to help him as much as he could."

"Why?"

"He—he once ran someone over and killed her, he—he always wanted to do everything he could to make amends, he—he felt guilty, although it wasn't his fault, everyone agreed that it wasn't his fault!"

"I've studied the evidence, and that makes it very clear," Roger reassured her. "Did Mr. Waite ever give you the drug?"

"No!"

"Did you first get the drug from the Campaign office?"

She didn't know what to answer, but stared at Gee and then turned away, as if she knew that this time she couldn't expect any help. Slowly he moved towards her, put a hand on her arm as if soothingly, and said in a voice which seemed a little lower-pitched: "Mrs. Cunliffe, if that is where you did get it from, you must tell the Chief Inspector – and tell me also. Because you might go back home and be persuaded to visit that apartment again, and if that's the source of your drug it would be fatal. We can't always make sure that we cure you, you know. Do you get the drug from there?"

Roger put in quietly, "The flat was destroyed by fire only last night. If that is where you've obtained it, you won't be able to go there again, so it won't help you to keep the information to yourself, Mrs. Cunliffe."

She raised her hands and her eyes seemed to bulge; then she took a step forward, pushing Gee aside. He kept close by her, as if to make sure that she didn't fling herself at Roger.

"Is that *true*? Has it been burned? *Has it?*"

"I saw it burn."

She turned away, buried her face in her hands, and cried, silently.

Judging from this, there seemed no possible doubt that she had got the drug from Waite's apartment.

"Please answer the question, Mrs. Cunliffe," Gee insisted shrilly, "and then I'm sure the Chief Inspector will be satisfied."

She didn't look up, but mumbled into her hands.

"Yes, I got it from the flat. I used to go once a fortnight and get it – there was a man there who gave me some for injection —" She couldn't go on.

Gee looked at Roger, not appealingly but commandingly.

"I think we must call that enough for the time being, Mr. West."

"Of course," Roger said quickly. "I needn't worry you any more, Mrs. Cunliffe, but thank you for being so helpful. Is there any message that I can give to Mr. Waite?"

Her face was haggard, her eyes hard and shiny with tears.

"No, nothing," she mumbled. "I—I've got such a terrible headache, I must—I must have some help." Her voice rose, and she turned on Gee: "I must have some help! Send for Dr. Smith, *I must have a little help!*"

That was how all addicts became. And if she had been ordered to name Waite, on pain of not receiving her shot, it would explain her cry of desperation now.

"Yes, yes, at once," said Gee. "I'll see Dr. Smith myself." He put a hand on Roger's arm and moved towards the door. "Just sit down and relax."

She stood watching, tense and desperate.

Roger let Gee stretch out his hand for the door handle, let him begin to open it, and then turned to look at the tragic woman, a ghost of beauty, and asked quietly and casually: "Have you had your photograph taken in the last few days, Mrs. Cunliffe?"

"Why, yes," she said. "I—I thought I was getting better. I had it taken for Ben, I—"

"And a *very* good one it was," interpolated Gee, "very good indeed." He drew Roger out of the room and closed the door, and they walked towards the landing and the head of a circular staircase. "Poor creature," Gee said, speaking in an unsteady voice, "in spite of all our efforts I am afraid her case is going to be a complete failure. I'm not at all sure that she ought to be allowed to go home, I shall have to talk to Dr. Smith about it. Mr. West, I wonder if you will be good enough to wait for me here, I won't keep you two or three minutes. I must arrange for Mrs. Cunliffe to have an injection."

He couldn't get away quickly enough, and went along another passage to a door marked *Private*.

Nothing he did or said could hide his nervousness – and that had been born the moment Roger had asked about the photograph.

The door closed on Gee, but his high-pitched voice seemed to echo about the landing, with the oil portraits on the wall, the thick pile carpet, the fine staircase leading down to the spacious hall. Up here were small tables, magazines, comfortable chairs, the air of opulence which struck one on entering the Clinic. But that wouldn't last. Gee was now a frightened man. He had made a fatal mistake – or someone had – in sending Mrs. Cunliffe's photograph to Jackson, but at the time there could have been no suspicion that the police would interview Mrs. Cunliffe.

The case should be over, soon – bar the shouting, and bar the understanding.

Roger could call the Yard from his car outside, close in the cordon, and start questioning Gee and Smith. It had to be done quickly. Gee couldn't have missed the significance of the question, he was almost certainly talking to Dr. Smith, *alias* Rawley, about the photograph and the questions, not about "help" for Mrs. Cunliffe.

Roger made for the head of the stairs, and hurried down. A well-dressed woman sat in the hall, looking through a magazine. He reached the front door and opened it without hindrance. His sergeant was parked at the side of the house, within a couple of minutes he could radio the request to the Yard, within minutes patrol cars would close in on the Palli Clinic.

He ran out on to the porch and the driveway.

The Yard car wasn't there.

Where it had stood there were two big ambulances.

"Looking for your car, sir?" asked an ambulance driver. "We had to ask all cars to park outside, plenty of room, sir – was yours the one with the chauffeur?"

"Yes."

"Just outside, sir."

"Thanks," said Roger.

The drive had seemed short, by car; on foot it seemed a mile long. Roger glanced round at the windows and the front door, but saw no one.

He stepped out of the drive, glancing right and left for his car. It was a little way off, but he couldn't see the driver. Suddenly, the engine of a nearby ambulance roared, and the ambulance surged forward.

## Chapter Twenty-Three

## Truth

The ambulance was no more than five yards away. It must have been on the move before Roger had appeared, it was coming too fast for a standing start. There was no time to think. Death came bearing down, so fast and so close that there did not seem any chance to escape it.

Roger had no time to fling himself forward, and if he tried to jump on to the bonnet he would simply add to the force of the impact. The ambulance seemed only feet away. He felt the warmth of the engine; and the roaring in his ears was shattering.

He flung himself backwards.

He was ready for the crack on the back of the head as he hit the ground, ready also for the hideous, crushing weight of the wheels. He struck the ground heavily, but his hat stayed on, and its crumpled brim lessened the force of the impact. Keeping his arms straight by his side, he stared up at the pulsing, oily bowels of the ambulance. He felt one wheel pinch his arm, saw the back wheels with an oblong of bright daylight beyond them.

Then the ambulance had passed over him.

He was hardly hurt, daylight almost blinded him, his heart hammered with dead fear. He felt paralysed, and there was no strength in him.

There was a different sound; a police whistle. Then he saw the Yard sergeant racing towards him, the whistle at his lips. The grocery van was coming, too. The engine of the ambulance was still loud, but getting fainter as it drew farther away. There was something near peacefulness out here, except for the rushing man and the hurtling car.

He mustn't lie here, but get *up. Get up.* No more proof was needed. Gee and Smith mustn't get away, no one must escape. Get *up.*

Roger began to struggle to his feet. His sergeant was very close.

"Block—both gateways," Roger called. The Flying Squad's laundry van was close, too. "Radio all cars. Hurry!" Head ringing, dizzy, wobbling badly, he started towards the van. "Key in that? Must block this gateway, must—hurry!" He fought off the dizziness and tried to run, but wasn't steady enough.

The Yard man said, "A dozen cars should be here in a minute."

"Nice work. Go round. Make sure the back exit's blocked."

He was at the door of the Yard car. He got in. The sergeant was already getting in beside the laundry-van driver, who was easing off the brake. Roger flicked the key round, and the ignition light glowed. He could imagine cars coming at speed along the drive, could picture them swinging out of the gateway. He started off. The gateway was only twenty yards away, but it seemed much farther, and he could hear engines whining.

He reached the gateway.

Three cars were coming from the side of the house – big, dark, shiny. He saw the driver of the first. Gee, and a younger man by his side. Roger jammed on the brakes in front of the exit, then he pushed open the door to jump out. But the cold hand of fear was upon him again, for Gee's car was coming too fast to stop before a crash. Roger leapt. He saw Gee's face, knew that the man was trying to stop, but hadn't a chance. The face of the younger man was gargoyle-like in its fear.

Roger was out of danger when he heard the crash of the impact. The impact was so savage that it looked as if the car he had jumped from would turn over; but it didn't. The nose of the big car had rammed it, and now looked like a concertina. A second car from the Clinic had crashed into the back of the first, and one man with blood all over his face was climbing out of the back, another man was slumped forward over the wheel.

Also in the back was Rosemary Jackson; unconscious.

The sergeant's message had reached the cordon cars, and they reached the scene before passers-by had started to extricate the victims. Rosemary Jackson did not seem to be hurt. Satisfied on that, Roger felt as if he had been given a shot in the arm.

"Now let's get a move on," he said to a car crew. "Check what's happened at the other entrance. Call the Yard, ask Superintendent Cortland to make sure that Benjamin Cunliffe doesn't take a walk, I want to talk to him." A sergeant was already calling the Yard by radio. "Ask the Yard for a dozen men, we want to go through that Clinic with a comb. As soon as more men arrive, have the place surrounded, and the grounds covered, too, we don't know what they might try next. And we want that garage at the back raided."

It would all get done; the problem was whether it would be done quickly enough.

When Roger was sure that no one else would be able to escape from the Palli Clinic, he went to see what was happening by the wreckage.

They'd got Gee out, and he was dead. Beside him was Dr. Smith, *alias* Rawley, also dead. Another man was badly injured, two only slightly hurt. All of the injured were being held, and police were detailed to go with them to the hospital.

A patrol-car man called to Roger, "Superintendent Cortland would like a word with you, sir."

"Right, thanks," said Roger, and moved over and took the receiver. "West here ... Eh? ... Yes, I should say it's all over, but we won't know until we've searched the place ... Looks to me as if the staff weren't involved, most of them knew nothing about it, but we'll see. I'm going to start going through the offices now ... Yes, tell Jackson his wife's all right ... Eh? ... Cunliffe, well, I wouldn't like to say I can prove he's in it deep, but I'll get a hell of a surprise if he isn't ... ever asked yourself if he *murdered* Mrs. Rawley? ... I may be crazy, I'll let you know," Roger said, and gave a tight-lipped grin.

"Send plenty of chaps over, Corty, it's a hell of a job here ... By the way, how's Waite?"

"Calm as you like, he's got a lot of guts," Cortland said "If he's clear, the sooner we can tell him the better I'll like it."

"Oh, he's clear," Roger said. "Tell June Akers, too."

He hurried to the Clinic in the wake of the C.I.D. men who had already arrived. The medical and domestic staff were being questioned, and most of them seemed completely bewildered. Roger didn't spend much time with them, but went to Mrs. Cunliffe's room; it was locked from the outside. He pushed the door open, and found her lying asleep on the bed.

"At least she's alive," he said to a sergeant, "have a man on duty here to make sure that she isn't disturbed. Anything found?"

They had found the room where Rosemary Jackson had been kept prisoner, the sergeant told him. According to the members of the staff, she had been a "patient" of Dr. Smith, and had been brought here in an ambulance; no one had suspected that she wasn't a genuine patient, here for a "cure". She had been attended only by Dr. Smith.

In the open fireplaces of Smith's *alias* Rawley's office, there were heaps of burned papers. The big safe in the office was open, and inside it and on the floor outside was a thick layer of white powder.

"Heroin or opium," Roger said with satisfaction. "They got supplies for the 'cure' purposes, kept it in the safe, and must have broken one of the containers while getting it away. The rest of the stuff will be in the wrecked cars." He sent a man to warn the police at the wreckage.

This was practically everything that he could do here.

He rang the Yard.

"I've been getting the reports," Cortland said with satisfaction. "It looks as if you've made a clean sweep, Handsome. Know the ins and outs of it all yet?"

"No, I'm just going to see Cunliffe, and when I've finished I hope to have the story," Roger said.

"He's still at his office."

"Good," said Roger. "Have someone telephone him – wait a minute, who've we got who's a good mimic? Middleton's not bad. Will you ask Middleton to wait for half an hour and then ring Cunliffe up? Tell him to use a falsetto voice – very high pitched, ventriloquist's dummy type of thing. He needn't be too particular. Have him tell Cunliffe that I've get on to his wife's photograph, and that he and the rest at the nursing home are on the run. Will you do that?"

"I don't know how you get away with it," said Cortland. "Chatworth must have spent half his time telling you not to be greedy. Okay."

"Thanks," said Roger, warmly.

Half an hour afterwards, with two C.I.D. men, he was outside the building in Portman Place where Benjamin Cunliffe had his office. His silver grey Rolls-Royce was double-parked, and ten minutes later he left the building.

He drove off, and Roger followed, with other police cars watching him all the way to the house near Regent's Park. Cunliffe left the Rolls-Royce and hurried indoors. Twenty minutes later he came out again. Roger, now in a different car, was at the corner. Cunliffe drove at a steady pace, towards Edgware Road, then across Hyde Park, and towards Hammersmith. Soon he was on the way to the London Airport. By radio, Roger kept the airport police informed.

A message was flashed back when they were a few minutes' drive from the airport.

"Aircraft leaving in half an hour for Paris, sir, and a Mr. Benjamin Cunliffe is due on board. The office has just received telephoned instructions to give him all facilities."

"I'll meet him at the aircraft," Roger said dryly.

Cunliffe came briskly, in line with the other passengers, giving no indication that he was alarmed or in flight. He carried a small briefcase, and his two suitcases had been loaded on to the trolley; the luggage was being put on to the aircraft. With the C.I.D. men and two airport police officers, Roger was waiting by the steps.

Roger stepped forward as Cunliffe drew up.

"Can you spare me a minute, Mr. Cunliffe?"

Cunliffe stopped in his tracks, opened his mouth and closed it again; when at last he managed to speak, his voice sounded thin and frightened.

"Why—why just now? I'm going on urgent business to Paris, what right have you—?"

"We'll have to ask you to postpone your trip," Roger said briskly. "There are a few questions we have to ask you. If you've satisfactory answers you can catch the next 'plane, sir."

Cunliffe looked as if he would faint.

With Roger by his side and the others bringing up the rear, he was led back to the airport buildings. A porter brought his luggage, and before he was questioned the luggage was opened and examined.

Cunliffe had been well prepared for an emergency get-away. He had large amounts of foreign currency folded inside various articles of clothing, a small fortune in diamonds spread about the cases – all easily negotiable wherever he went. He had letters of credit for substantial sums, and there were statements from foreign banks showing that, under different names, he had accumulated credit balances in several different countries.

There was also one small container of heroin.

"What have you charged him with?" Cortland asked Roger, when Roger was back at the Yard late that afternoon. "You could pretty well take your pick."

"Haven't formally charged him with anything yet," said Roger, "but there's one charge in particular that I'd like to make stick."

"Which one?"

"The murder of Mrs. Rawley, remember?" said Roger. "I think he drove at her deliberately, it wasn't an accident. I think Rawley knew that it wasn't, too; I think that Rawley, a pharmaceutical chemist with access to dangerous drugs like heroin, was already in the dope traffic, with Cunliffe. I think that Rawley's wife found out, and that after reasoning with her husband and finding that he wouldn't stop it, she was going to inform the police. And I think that all the witnesses were fixed. The one that's going to hurt us is Atkinson. Remember Atkinson came into a small fortune just after the affair, and applied for a transfer to Totting, where he bought his house. I think we'll find that he bought it with the money he got for giving false evidence."

Cortland said slowly, "I'm beginning to see daylight, Handsome, but where do the others come in?"

"I know I'm sticking my neck out," said Roger, "but now that Brown's talked a bit, I can put two and two together with some explanations. Brown's been with Rawley for several years – he and the other dope-runners did it first for the money, then for the dope itself. They all became addicts. So far as I can see, this is how it went:

"Mrs. Bray had been working for Rawley ever since the Ligate accident case. She was a regular Campaign helper. Atkinson gave her, and Brown, and the other members of the gang who used the Campaign office as a cover, any protection they needed. Then Mrs. Bray and Atkinson became over-confident; they knew so much about Rawley and what he was doing as 'Dr. Smith', that they felt they could safely take some of the dope, break with the Palli Clinic and set up their own organisation. They knew all the addicts who called regularly at the Campaign office, so they'd ready-made customers. Brown says that they undercut Rawley's price, and so took his business.

"Rawley didn't dare give them away, but had to stop them. The only way was to kill. First he killed Mrs. Bray, and that probably kept Atkinson quiet for a bit, although he might not have realised that she was murdered. Then another, totally unexpected thing happened to frighten Rawley; Charles Jackson, also involved in the old Ligate case, saw him at the Palli Clinic. I fancy that was the time when Rawley knew that his game was up. From then on, he could hope only to get away with what he had. But there was danger all round. Jackson was one source, and he had to be controlled. The obvious way was to get some hold over him, and Rawley tried that through his wife. The plot against the Jacksons began before the other troubles came to a head, and failed because circumstances compelled Rawley to act too quickly; had he been worried only about the

Jacksons and Atkinson, he would probably have got away with it – at least for a while.

"But for years he had prepared a way of keeping himself in the clear. He had worked with Waite as unwitting cover, and thought the frame-up was foolproof.

"What he hadn't foreseen was trouble with Mrs. Kitt.

"There was nothing remarkable in Mrs. Kitt getting in touch with Waite; in fact, it was a logical development of her attitude. The irony was in the fact that Mrs. Kitt rebelled, and so really let us in.

"Brown went to kill her, and left her for dead. But there was Atkinson still to worry about, and the need to put the finishing touches to the framing of Waite. Jackson had to be dealt with, too, especially when it was known that he was employing an inquiry agent. Rawley had undoubtedly planned one job at a time, but it didn't work out, and soon it became all or nothing. At one go.

"He planned a swift series of murders, using Brown each time – Brown had already killed Mrs. Bray.

"First, Jackson was to go. But Jackson escaped death, and his wife was kidnapped in a desperate attempt to keep him quiet. We know the consequences of that.

"Next came Atkinson's turn. He died.

"Then, there was Waite.

"I've little doubt that if we hadn't got on to Waite when we did, he would have been killed, and posthumously 'proved' to have been the drug-distributor, so taking the heat off Rawley," Roger went on. "But when we were known to be after Waite, it couldn't be done so simply. Waite had all those names and addresses of Rawley's customers, and they had to be destroyed; Rawley daren't let us get them. Waite would carry most of them in his head, too, so he still had to die.

"We know how narrowly he escaped.

"We can guess how desperate Rawley was, from the moment he knew that Mrs. Kitt and Jackson were alive. But he couldn't stop, he had to keep trying. Brown was in too deep to back out, and there was always the hope that we'd see Waite as the killer."

"Not a forlorn hope, either," Cortland said dryly. "Some of us did. How much of this do you think we can prove?"

"We can prove all we need to," Roger said. "Cunliffe will probably try to put all the blame on Gee and Rawley, as they're dead, but a man who could turn his own wife into a dopey can't have that much luck."

"See that he doesn't," urged Cortland.

Roger left him and went downstairs to see Cunliffe, who had been cooling his heels for some time. He jumped to his feet as Roger entered, and burst out before anything was said: "I simply couldn't help myself, West! I was being blackmailed. I'd worked with Rawley years ago, and he had his claws in me. He—*he* fixed my wife, West, I couldn't stop—"

"You didn't do a thing to help her," Roger said coldly. "It would have been kinder to have killed her, as you killed Mrs. Rawley."

"West! That's a lie, that—"

"Mr. Cunliffe, there is one thing you don't know," said Roger, icily. "Since the deaths of Sergeant Atkinson and Mrs. Bray, we have sufficient grounds for establishing that they gave false evidence at your trial after the so-called accident which killed Mrs. Rawley. We shall proceed with that investigation. We have also found documents at the Palli Clinic which establish your part in the supplying and distributing of dangerous drugs. If you make a full and detailed statement, it may help you. Nothing else can."

"Oh, God," Cunliffe groaned. "I—I tell you I was being blackmailed, West. It was this way …"

His statement, which he signed later in the day, dotted the 'i's and crossed the 't's of Roger's talk to Cortland. It was all there: how Mrs. Bray and Atkinson, breaking away, had started the rot, how Rawley and Cunliffe had been compelled to fight against time, how the Government's inquiry had made difficulties, how Jackson …

As he drove home that evening, Roger wondered if Cunliffe would have broken down so completely if he'd known that the "evidence" about false witness about Mrs. Rawley's death was negligible.

Ethically, that trick had been all wrong.

Ethically, he was a bad policeman

Certainly, it had been a hell of a case. You got to wondering what was the real drug – heroin and opium or the money that could buy people like Cunliffe, Atkinson and Mrs. Bray. But there were the good things. Mrs. Cunliffe would really be cured, the Jacksons would go back to the honeymoon stage, and Mrs. Kitt's part would stay in the archives, but never become public.

Peter Waite's luck was on the turn, too. There was June's steadfastness and loyalty to help him; it wouldn't be long before the fire was in his belly again.

Mrs. Atkinson and her Betty would have a rough time, but – P.C. Davis had a shoulder for them to lean on. First-class man, Davis, better even than Pye; both good, though, and soon to be transferred to the plain-clothes branch.

The case apart, Roger had every reason to be more light-hearted, for the news was spreading at the Yard that Chatworth had turned the corner. There'd have to be a new Assistant Commissioner; Chatworth wasn't likely to come back to duty, but it was one thing to think of him in retirement, another to think of him as dead.

Roger reached Bell Street, garaged the car, and went into the empty house. It was time Janet was back; you didn't realise how much you took a wife for granted until she had gone away for a while. The boys, too. And at least he wouldn't forget to telephone them tonight!

He took the evening newspapers from the door, glanced through them, and then stared down at a big front page spread in the *Globe*.

He read:

The *Evening Globe* believes that in his passionate campaigning against the slaughter – he rightly uses the word murder – on the roads of our fair country, the Reverend Peter Waite has been truly serving the cause of the people. After learning of the tragic uses to which his Campaign Headquarters were being put, and hearing that fire destroyed everything but the spirit of his campaign, the *Evening Globe* proposes to espouse this cause, with Mr. Waite as its leader.

The people of this country must be made to realise that the senseless slaughter on the roads must and can be stopped – that whoever is to blame must be severely punished. Fear, as Mr. Waite makes clear, is the only weapon which can be used against the appalling carelessness which costs so many human lives.

June Akers would discipline Parson Pete, Roger reflected; she would check the wilder extravagances, and would help to streamline this campaign so that it began to influence the people.

Anyhow, she would try.

Roger finished his supper, washed up and saw that it was half-past nine. He was tired of waiting, so he picked up the telephone and put a call through to his wife.

# JOHN CREASEY

## GIDEON'S DAY

Gideon's day is a busy one. He balances family commitments with solving a series of seemingly unrelated crimes from which a plot nonetheless evolves and a mystery is solved.

One of the most senior officers within Scotland Yard, George Gideon's crime solving abilities are in the finest traditions of London's world famous police headquarters. His analytical brain and sense of fairness is respected by colleagues and villains alike.

'The finest of all Scotland Yard series' – New York Times.

## GIDEON'S FIRE

Commander George Gideon of Scotland Yard has to deal successively with news of a mass murderer, a depraved maniac, and the deaths of a family in an arson attack on an old building south of the river. This leaves little time for the crisis developing at home ....

'Gideon of Scotland Yard emerges as one of the most real working detectives in modern fiction.... A sympathetic and believable professional policeman.' - New York Times

# JOHN CREASEY

## THE CREEPERS

"The prisoner's hand was thin and bony ... And in the centre of the palm was a pinkish mark. It was the shape of a wolf's head, mouth open, fangs showing. Although it was what he had expected to see, Inspector West felt a twinge of repugnance a stab not unrelated to fear. It was the fifth time he had seen the mark of the wolf – the mark of Lobo."

A gang of cat burglars led by Lobo cause mayhem as they terrorize the city. They must be stopped, but with little in the way of evidence the police are baffled. Just how can Inspector West manage to do this in what is a race against time before more victims succumb?

*"Here is an excellent novel of law enforcement officers, harried, discouraged and desperately fatigued, moving inexorably ahead under the pressure of knowledge that they must succeed to save human lives." - Cleveland Plain-Dealer*

*"Furiously exciting" - Chicago Tribune*

*"The action is fast, continuous and exciting" - San Francisco News*

# John Creasey

## The House of the Bears

Standing alone in the bleak Yorkshire Moors is Sir Rufus Marne's 'House of the Bears'. Dr. Palfrey is asked to journey there to examine an invalid - who has now disappeared. Moreover, Marne's daughter lies terribly injured after a fall from the minstrel's gallery which Dr. Palfrey discovers was no accident. He sets out to investigate and the results surprise even him . . . .

*"'Palfrey' and his boys deserve to take their places among the immortals." - Western Mail*

## Introducing the Toff

Whilst returning home from a cricket match at his father's country home, the Honourable Richard Rollison - alias The Toff - comes across an accident which proves to be a mystery. As he delves deeper into the matter with his usual perseverance and thoroughness, murder and suspense form the backdrop to a fast moving and exciting adventure.

*'The Toff has been promoted to a place of honour among amateur detectives.' – The Times Literary Supplement*

Printed in Poland
by Amazon Fulfillment
Poland Sp. z o.o., Wrocław